OUTPOST EPSILON

A STONEWALL CHRONICLES
NOVEL

HERBERT GROSSHANS

OUTPOST EPSILON
Copyright © 2018 by Herbert Grosshans

ISBN: 978-1-68046-687-4

Melange Books, LLC
White Bear Lake, MN 55110
www.melange-books.com

Published in the United States of America.

Cover Design by Ashley Redbird Designs

THE STONEWALL CHRONICLES NOVELS

TERREX STONEWALL SHOULDERED HIS HUGE DUFFLE BAG, WHICH held his meager possessions, and stepped from the shuttle onto the alien soil. Taking a deep breath, he inhaled the hot, humid air, registering unfamiliar scents and finding them not as unpleasant as he'd been told.

The door of the shuttle irised shut behind him, cutting off his way back should he change his mind about this new assignment, and he moved further away as the small shuttle lifted into the air. It rose then disappeared into the low hanging clouds.

Although he had been briefed, it still came as a surprise to see the giant mushrooms surrounding him. He walked slowly across the cleared area toward the enormous bubble that would be his home for the next year.

He knew what to expect.

Life on an outpost was not a holiday. Neither did it mean hardship, not usually. His job, as a scout for the Solar Union, would be to keep watch over this area of space and report any intrusion into the system.

They did not tell him why this particular outpost was so important. Epsilon happened to be the fourth planet in a solar system at the edge of controlled Human Space. There wasn't much here, as far as Stonewall knew. Nothing anyone would want, unless you liked mushrooms.

The shrill cry of an animal hastened his steps toward the dome. Before he reached it, an opening appeared in the smooth surface of the bubble, and a man in the drab brown uniform of the Union stepped out.

"No canvassing allowed." The man burst out laughing when he saw Stonewall's perplexed expression. Holding out a hand, he said, "You must be Terrex Stonewall. I am William Peters. Welcome to Hell."

"Hell?" Stonewall said. Then he nodded and grinned, suddenly aware of the wet fabric of his uniform clinging to his perspiring body. "It is damned hot."

"Come inside." The other man stepped back into the dome.

Stonewall followed him and stood silent for a moment, breathing in the cool air. Behind him, the door closed with a barely audible *whoosh*.

From the outside, the surface of the dome looked opaque, but standing inside, he could see the sky above and the forest of mushrooms as clearly as if the shell didn't exist.

"Pretty clever," he commented.

"It is. Don't ask me how it's done. I'm not a scientist. Something about bending the light waves."

"You even have a garden," Stonewall observed.

"That and more. Makes living on this hell-hole almost bearable." Peters pointed to a squat building. "Those are our sleeping quarters. The kitchen and mess hall are over there. That ugly structure behind the kitchen houses the observation screens, computers, and detection systems. Below it, underground, is the power grid. We call that building the Power-building." He grinned. "Very original, don't you agree? You'll be spending most of your time in there."

Stonewall saw a couple of figures moving around in the garden. Peters noticed his interest. "Don't worry," he said, laughing. "You won't have to work in the garden. Those are work-drones. Robots."

Stonewall grinned. "You had me worried there for a moment. I'm not a farmer."

"Speaking of farmers," Peters said, "there is the Chief right now. His name is..."

"Derrol Farmer. I know." Stonewall smiled.

The tall man who came walking toward them, looked gaunt, like someone who hadn't slept or eaten for days. "So, you're the new guy," he said with a grating voice, giving Stonewall a tight smile.

"The name's Terrex Stonewall, sir."

"I'm aware of that. Call me *Chief*. We are not that formal around here." Farmer pointed at Stonewall's duffel bag. "What did you bring with you? I hope all that stuff fits into your locker." He stared at Peters. "Show him his bunk and introduce him to the others."

Peters tipped his non-existent helmet in a sloppy salute. "Will do, Chief."

Farmer turned and walked away.

"Is he always in this cheerful mood?" Stonewall asked when he was out of earshot.

Peters chuckled. "Not always. Today is one of his better days." He punched Stonewall on the arm. "Come, I'll show you to your executive suite."

He took Stonewall to the dormitory and showed him his bunk. "Here we are. Your lavish quarters for the next year." He grinned. "Just throw your stuff on the bed. You can stow it away later. It's almost noon, but before we go for lunch, I want you to see your new workplace."

When they entered the Power-building, Terrex smelled the sterile air, like the air in a hospital ward. "These instruments are quite delicate. They don't like dust or temperature fluctuations. Better put on one of the lab coats." Peters handed him a white coat. Then they walked down a short tunnel and through a door into a large room full of computers and electronic devices.

"Transmissions from the satellites circling Epsilon," Peters said, pointing at the screens covering one wall. They displayed images of stars and empty space.

Only four of the computer terminals were occupied. One of the men looked up when Peters approached. "Hey, Peters," he said. Glancing at Stonewall, he nodded. "The new guy?"

"Yep. Terrex Stonewall meet Ferd Prowler. He's the supervisor on this shift. He'll be *your* supervisor."

"Hey, Stonewall," Prowler said. "Welcome to *Shithole*. I hope you'll be happy here."

Stonewall smiled and lifted his hand. "Hey."

Prowler's expression turned serious, and he looked at Peters. "Better call the Chief. I've lost contact with Wong and Maisoneuve."

"What the fuck are you saying?"

"I'm saying that I've lost contact with Wong and Maisoneuve, you dimwit. The beacon of the rover died an hour ago, and I can't raise them on their personal comm. Haven't been able for a couple of days now, but I thought maybe their comms were faulty. We've been having trouble with them for quite some time now. I didn't think anything of it."

"Fuck it!" Peters cursed again. "The Chief won't be happy." He grabbed Stonewall's arm. "Come with me. Maybe your presence will keep him from executing me on the spot for being the bearer of bad news."

"What happened?" Stonewall asked as he walked beside Peters.

"A few days ago, we tracked an intruder into the system. A small ship of unknown origin. We got a fairly good image of it as it passed one of our surveillance drones. It traveled much too fast as it entered the ionosphere of this planet. And the angle was wrong, too. It crashed not far from here. We sent out two of our people to search for the ship and see if there were any survivors. They've been out there now for three days."

He glanced at Stonewall. "This place might look peaceful and exotic with all those giant mushrooms, like a scene out of a fairy tale, but believe me, appearances are deceiving, literally. Danger lurks everywhere. On the ground and in the air. Even underground. You don't want to be caught out there without a protective suit and a flash-rifle in each hand."

Chief Farmer stayed surprisingly calm when Peters gave him the news. "We'll have to send a team to find them," he said, his voice barely above a whisper. "If anything happened to them, there'll be hell to pay. Prowler should have notified me the minute he couldn't contact them on their coms."

Since Stonewall was the junior scout, Chief Farmer decided to have him accompany Peters on the rescue mission.

"You two seem to have hit it off," he said. "You'll make a good team." He gave Stonewall a long look. "Might as well get christened with fire, Stonewall. You're not here for a holiday. Begin earning your pay."

"Yes, sir," Stonewall said, not sure if he liked his assignment.

"I told you don't call me *sir*. I'm the Chief, understood?" Farmer didn't raise his voice but Stonewall felt a cold shiver running down his spine when he looked into the gaunt man's eyes.

"I understand, Chief," he said, cowering a little, wondering if Farmer would draw his sidearm and shoot him if he protested too much.

"You'll leave at dawn tomorrow. No sense in searching now. You'll want to cross *Dragon's gap* in the early hours."

"Dragon's gap?" Stonewall asked Peters after they left the Chief's office.

"You'll see when we get there," Peters said, evasively. "Let's grab something to eat."

Stonewall met the rest of the twelve scouts still on the station, all seven of them, including the four who manned the observation tower outside the bubble. All were young, in their twenties, like Stonewall. He also met the cook, Tommy, and his helper Garth, a small, skinny guy with eyes like a weasel.

"He's not too smart," Peters told him later and, grinning, he added, "The rumor has it that he and Tommy do more than just cooking in the backroom, if you know what I mean. But that's just that, rumors. Don't quote me."

Not all of the twelve men were in their beds at night, since they worked shifts around the clock in the tower and the Power building. The nightshift consisted of only two men instead of four.

It seemed Stonewall had barely fallen asleep when someone shook his shoulder. Bolting upright, he stared bleary-eyed at Peters.

"Time to get up," Peters whispered.

"Already?" Stonewall rubbed his eyes. "But it's still dark."

"Not outside. The sun is already up. Come, get dressed."

One hour later, they left the safety of the dome, dressed in protective clothing and flash-rifles slung across their shoulders.

Peters mounted one of the two scooters and Stonewall climbed into the sidecar. Then they took off into the mushroom jungle.

"How do you know in which direction to drive?" Stonewall asked. Through the built-in speaker of his helmet he could hear Peters chuckling cheerfully.

"We've sent out a *Seeker* to find the crashed alien ship. It is still hovering above the ship, sending a beacon. The locater on this scooter zeros in on the beacon. Our boys should be somewhere on the road to that location, unless they strayed off. Then we might have a problem finding them."

Stonewall didn't have to ask Peters to explain the *Seeker,* a tiny robotic spy-eye no larger than a marble, but capable of finding anything that contained electronic devices. Some called it a *Bloodhound.* A shame it couldn't find people.

He studied the environment they traveled in. Giant mushrooms rose on either side, some with thick stems and wide umbrellas, some thin, like trees, topped only with a small round bulb. Millions of tiny mushrooms grew from the soft ground, which was covered by a mat of blue-shimmering moss-like vegetation. Occasionally they passed beds of red low-growing shrubs.

Peters avoided these shrubs with deliberate care. "Those branches have razor-sharp thorns that could penetrate even our protective clothing. Besides, they are a favorite hiding place for the *Fire-spitters*."

"Fire-spitters?"

"Serpents with huge heads. If you come too close, they spit a wad of acid in your face. Won't kill you but burns like hell."

After traveling for an hour, they left the forest of mushrooms and came upon a wide stretch of bare rock.

"Dragon's gap." Peters stopped the scooter. "It's still early, but you never know. Those *Ants* are predictable, but not so the occasional *Anteater* who lies waiting for them, or the Dragons hovering in the sky, hoping for an easy snack." He unstrapped his flash-rifle.

"You're talking in riddles. Remember, I'm new here." Stonewall twisted his neck, searching the sky for signs of life. "I don't see anything."

"The *Ants* are giant...well...ants, as big as sheep. Every day, shortly after noon, an army of them travels across this parcel of land. They return just before dark. Where they go and what they do is unknown to us. They seem harmless enough, and they won't pursue you if you're not too close, but they don't hesitate to attack if they feel threatened."

"What about the Anteater?"

"Fierce beasts the size of an elephant with six long spidery legs. They eat Ants."

"Humans?"

Peters chuckled. "And Humans. So do the *Dragons*. If you remember what a pterodactyl looks like, you'll have an idea of the type of creature I'm talking about. They sail the currents above, looking for a bite to eat."

"Any other beasties I need to know about?"

"Well...there are the giant *Lice, Beetles, Seed-crackers*. All of them live in the mushrooms. The *Earth-borers, the Cave-borers, the Excavators, the...*"

Stonewall held up a hand. "I get the point. In other words, *watch your step*."

"All the time. Never let down your guard. Expect the unexpected, even when you're convinced everything is safe. It never is. That's why we live in the bubble. The only safe place on this planet. For Humans."

"I think I want to go back now." Stonewall grinned, even though he knew Peters couldn't see his face. Unfortunately, it was not far from the truth.

"You and I both," Peters said. "Keep your eyes open."

The scooter began moving again. Slowly, they drove out onto the barren land.

When Stonewall saw the giant shadow on the ground, saw it increasing in size with alarming speed, he knew they had only seconds left. He brought up his rifle, twisted in his seat, almost froze when he saw the huge shape scooping down on them.

The explosive sound of a flash-rifle discharging beside him embarrassed him, knowing that his partner had been faster in dealing with the danger. However, he didn't have much time to think about it. Pulling the trigger on his own weapon, he watched as the searing bolt of energy buried itself in the chest of the giant reptilian predator.

Screaming defiantly, it desperately tried to rise again, flapping its great wings but failed when Peters sliced off half of one wing with a sweep of his rifle.

As the beast crashed to the ground behind them, Peters gunned the scooter, raced away from the screeching mortally wounded creature. "Hang on!" he called out.

Stonewall held on to his rifle, keeping an eye on their surroundings.

A dark form, as large as a shuttle, came scuttling out of a deep crevice in the ground, but it ignored them and headed for the convulsing body of the *Dragon*.

"It's our lucky day," Peters said. "That Anteater would have ambushed us, but we supplied it with an easier meal, that and much more meat."

They reached the other side of *Dragon's gap* unmolested and entered another forest.

"Don't relax yet," Peters warned. "This is where we usually encounter the *Seed-crackers*. They live in the gills of the mushrooms and like to drop onto unwary travelers. They're small, but their mandibles are sharp and strong. Some of the boys call them *Piranhas*.

One is not much of a threat, but a swarm of them can cut you into tiny pieces in a short time."

Stonewall's skin felt clammy from perspiring inside his protective suit. Even though a battery-powered tiny cooling unit in his helmet removed some of the moisture from the air he breathed through a set of filters, it still seemed uncomfortably hot.

"Can we take a short break?" he asked. "I need to stretch my legs. There isn't much room in this bullet I'm sitting in."

"All right." Peters appeared reluctant. "But just for a short time. I could use some stretching myself." He stopped and dismounted but kept his rifle in his hand, ready to be used in an instant.

Stonewall climbed out of the sidecar and walked around, trying to get the cramps out of his aching legs. "I never asked. Do you have any contact with the indigenous people on Epsilon?"

Peters laughed. "Count yourself lucky if we don't run into them. They are not very friendly. The *Bugeyes* and Humans don't get along."

"How much do we know about them?"

"Not much. We know they live in hives. They build huge mounds, like the termites on Earth, only on a grander scale. They seem quite intelligent, but as I said, we aren't exactly on friendly terms with them."

Even through the filter, Stonewall could still smell the decaying odor of fungus. "Strange world," he muttered.

Peters chuckled. "Epsilon is not a world created for us Humans. We are intruders here. Humans will never live here." He scanned the sky, visible above the giant umbrellas. "We'd better get a move-on. I don't trust this part of the forest."

3

THEY FOUND THE ROVER SHORTLY AFTER NOON. NO SIGN OF THE two missing scouts. The exit door to the rover stood open, the instruments a jumble of broken gauges and ripped-out wires.

"Bugeyes!" Peters cursed. He began searching the ground for tracks. "Yeah, there must have been a whole troop of them. Probably surprised Wong and Maisoneuve when they left the rover to take a leak or something. Maisoneuve always had a small bladder."

Stonewall saw an object on the ground, behind a clump of purple shrubbery.

A helmet.

"What do you think happened to them?" he asked.

Peters shrugged. "Your guess is as good as mine. We've never had any serious clashes with the Bugeyes. We're under direct orders never to shoot at them or behave in any way that could be construed as threatening." He took the helmet from Stonewall. "This belongs to Maisoneuve. I can tell by the letter *M* etched into the left side." He shook his head. "Why would he take off his helmet?"

Wong's helmet lay not far away. Stonewall picked it up and studied it. He couldn't find any signs of it being removed forcefully. No blood on the inside, nor did he notice any damage to the helmet itself. "Do you think they're dead?" he asked.

"I hope not." Peters walked back to the disabled rover and looked inside. "Their rifles are still on the backseat," he said. "Those fools! How could they have been so careless?" Unslinging his rifle from his back, he warned Stonewall, "Be on guard."

Stonewall scanned the darkness inside the mushroom forest. The buzzing of insects and chirping of other small critters seemed suddenly loud in his ears. When he saw movement beside one of the thick stems, he brought up his rifle, but it was only a huge beetle-like creature scuttling on multiple legs toward the top of the mushroom tree.

"What's going to happen now?" he asked.

"As far as Wong and Maisoneuve are concerned? Nothing. We have to assume they're beyond help. There is nothing we can do to help them. They're on their own."

"We can't just abandon them!"

"What do you suggest?" Peters gave him a hard stare. "Go after them?"

"Well..." Stonewall made a helpless gesture.

"Tell me which way! I'm not a tracker." Peters sounded almost hysterical. "To us, they're dead." He kicked one of the low growing mushrooms. It burst with a loud pop and released a cloud of red spores. "Fuck it! Fuck it!" he cursed. "I hate this whole fucking place!"

Stomping over to the rover, he closed the door by slamming it harder than necessary. "Let's hope nobody decided to take up residence in there."

"What about the rifles?" Stonewall asked.

"We'll leave them. They'll be safe in there. We can't carry them. If the *Bugeyes* had wanted the rifles, they would have taken them." Peters gave the rover another look. "I'd better call it in. The Chief will want to salvage this vehicle as soon as possible. Benjamin and Purdue will have to examine it. They're good at fixing things. Let's not waste any more time. I want to get to the crash site before it gets dark."

Ten minutes later, they were on their scooter, following the beacon from the *Seeker*. Stonewall sat in the sidecar, feeling depressed. This was only the second day of his yearlong tour of duty, and already he felt sorry for even thinking about signing up for it. He should have gone to Alpha Centauri, as his father suggested. There he would have been able to walk around without all of this protective clothing and facemask. The air on *Erde*, the second planet of Alpha Centauri, apparently always smelled as fresh as the air on a clear day in spring on Earth.

But no, he wanted to see the far frontiers, experience adventure, see new things!

Fuck that whim! Fuck the Scouts!

He should have become a button pusher, like his brother Helm. Not much adventure there, but at least it was a safe job.

The surroundings seemed more foreboding and gloomier than before. He saw movements behind every mushroom stem, shadows hiding inside every shrub they passed. His fingers hurt from holding his flash-rifle too tight, and his legs seemed rigid pieces of wood without feelings inside the cramped interior of the sidecar.

Fuck it!

He must have dozed off. A loud curse and the sound of rifle fire made him jerk up his head. They were racing across the soft ground, and he almost lost the grip on his rifle.

"Stonewall!" Peters' voice sounded loud in his ears. "What the hell are you doing? Are you sleeping? You're supposed to keep watch."

Stonewall turned his head to look back. Behind them trotted a creature out of someone's nightmare. He remembered seeing pictures of creatures like that in schoolbooks. But they were extinct on Earth for millions of years. Obviously not on this planet. Nothing surprised him anymore.

"What the fuck is that?" he yelled, instantly alert.

"Dinosaur," Peters yelled back.

"What do you want me to do?"

"Shoot the bastard. Damn it, Stonewall! Didn't they teach you anything?"

Stonewall twisted his body, aimed his rifle at the behemoth but had difficulty keeping it steady because of the uneven ground they raced across.

The beast closed the distance between them. A loud roar escaped from its open maw. Stonewall couldn't help but notice the long, dagger-like teeth and huge claws on the powerful hind legs.

He managed to get the broad scaly chest in his viewfinder and pulled the trigger.

Missed! Fuck it!

His second shot hit the creature square in the chest. It stumbled but kept on going. He fired another shot, missed again. The next shot burnt off one of the short front legs. It didn't slow down the by now enraged beast.

Finally, he put a lucky shot between the snapping jaws and shouted triumphantly when the giant dinosaur faltered and crashed to the ground. The long thick tail pounded the soft forest floor, but he knew this nightmare creature wouldn't get up again.

"Got it!" he hollered, laughing hysterically.

"You're sure?"

"I'm sure. That sucker is done for. Food for the beetles and other nasties that live on this forsaken planet."

Peters slowed down and looked back. "These guys are tough. Not that easy to kill."

"Can we expect more of those?" Stonewall felt suddenly weak, as the adrenalin rush abated. He wanted to wipe his forehead, but just managed to touch the top of his helmet.

"This is the second one I've seen," Peters said. "Luckily, the first one was far away. Prowler and a couple of the boys had a run-in with one similar to this one, but not quite as huge. They had a hell of a time killing it."

"I think I'll have to go for a piss. Can we stop?"

"Sure, I wouldn't mind having a bite to eat and drink some water. We'll stop in a few minutes. I'd like to put some distance between this mountain of meat and us. It will attract others, maybe even bigger monsters."

They stopped after a few minutes and dismounted. Peters unpacked some sandwiches and handed a bottle of water to Stonewall who accepted it gratefully. Taking off his helmet, he finally managed to wipe his perspiring forehead. The humid, stifling air took away his breath for a short moment, but then his system adjusted, and he inhaled the overpowering scents of the alien forest.

"Can you ever get used to this?" he asked.

Peters chuckled. "You can get used to anything, Stonewall. We

Humans are quite adaptable, but who would want to get used to this?" He munched on his sandwich. "You ever been to *Easter*?"

"Never heard of it."

"You probably know it as Y25, the closest planet of Barnard's Star. The sky there is always red and not very bright, but it's beautiful. Very romantic. My dad took me there when I was just a kid. He was in the mining business, you know."

"How can you know it was romantic if you were just a kid?"

"I heard the rich people go there for their honeymoon. The gravity is less than on Earth. Apparently, sex is very satisfying in lower gravity." He chuckled. "Do you have someone waiting for you when you get back?"

Stonewall thought of Lucinda, bitter memories rising in him. She was partially the reason for his decision to come to this damned place. Women! They say one thing and mean another. While she told him she loved only him, she screwed her cousin Danny more often than him. "No," he said. "Nobody."

"I have a wife and a little boy waiting for me."

"You're married?"

"Yes, I am. That's why I'm here. To earn some money. It'll give me and my wife a good start."

"How long have you been here?"

"Ten months. I'll be going home in two." Peters drained his bottle. Stowing it in the storage compartment behind his seat, he grinned and said, "Do you know what's going to be the first thing I'll do when I get home?"

"Make love to your wife?" Stonewall smiled.

"That will be the second thing I'll do. No, the very first thing I'll do is have a bottle of beer, maybe even two or three. There is no alcohol allowed here on the station. You know that, don't you?"

Stonewall shrugged. "I didn't know, but it doesn't bother me. I don't drink alcohol."

"No shit? Do you fuck?"

"What?" Stonewall shook his head, the question taking him by surprise. "What kind of a stupid question is that?"

Peters chuckled. "A very good question, my friend who doesn't drink. Probably don't smoke, either. You've got no woman waiting for you." He squinted at Stonewall. "Do you like men?"

"Do I like men? You mean am I a homosexual?"

"That's what I mean."

Stonewall gave Peters an intent stare. "What if I am?"

"Wouldn't bother me, as long as you don't bother me."

"Well, don't worry about that. I'm straight. I like women, don't care much for gay men. Happy?"

Peters slapped his shoulder. "I actually don't care one way or the other, but you'll have to put a knot in that pecker of yours. There are no women on Epsilon." A loud drumming from nearby, answered by another from somewhere above them, made him look around. "*Bloodfrogs*," he said. "We'd better get a move on. One of those critters can suck the blood out of your veins faster than you can say *Mommy*."

4

The alien ship lay partially submerged in a swampy area of the forest. When it came down it had cut a wide swath into a patch of low-growing mushroom trees, finally coming to rest in the cushioning bed of reed-like grass.

They left the scooter in the protection of the forest and approached the vessel carefully.

"I don't recognize the design," Peters said as they slowly walked through the high grass toward the oval-shaped vessel.

"Neither do I. One thing I'm sure of, it's not a *Dragon*-designed shuttle, neither was it built by the *Crows*." Stonewall tried to recall all of the different races Humans encountered so far.

Dragons, as they called the reptilian races. He knew of seven or eight different sub-species. Their ships were ugly, square and bulky. The *Crows*, whose ancestors had been birds, built ships with delicate lines, beautiful to look at. Then there were the *Spiders*, a non-humanoid race from the red giant Arcturus. They flew in ships that looked spidery and flowing. And menacing.

There were others, but he didn't know all of them.

This shuttle looked almost like a giant egg. It had split open at impact. They didn't see any signs of life.

"Be careful," Peters warned. "They may be lying in wait for a meal or something. And don't forget to watch where you step. There are sinkholes in this swamp. This place is a favorite hiding place for *Bullfish*. They could be anywhere." He held his rifle ready to be fired in an instant.

Stonewall walked beside him. Every step he took seemed an effort, as his boots sank deep into the soft bog. He gripped the cool metal of his weapon with clammy hands. "I don't think anyone is alive in there," he ventured. "It's been a couple of days now."

Peters looked back at the forest and then at the swath the ship had cut. "They sure came down fast. I'm surprised it didn't explode."

A loud piercing cry prompted Stonewall to look up. A few dark shapes circled above them in the cloudy sky. Peters noticed his look. He chuckled without humor.

"The vultures are already gathering. But don't worry, they only like dead meat."

The exit door to the vessel stood open. Peters put a hand against Stonewall's chest. Shaking his head, he whispered, "Someone made it out of that door. He might be hiding close by. Search the area. I'll keep watch."

Stonewall walked slowly in small circles, searching the high grass for bodies. He didn't think he'd find anyone living.

When he stumbled over the lifeless body of one of the travelers, he called out, "I found someone."

Peters came to stand beside him. He prodded the body with his foot, but it didn't move. "Looks like he's dead," he said.

The alien looked humanoid, dressed in a drab gray uniform. He didn't wear a helmet. Stonewall bent down and turned the body around so they could look at the face.

"He looks human," Peters commented, "but he's not. His ears are too small, and his nose too flat. He doesn't have any eyebrows." He stared at the open eyes. "Slit pupils, like a cat. Nope, definitely not human."

Stonewall didn't remember ever seeing pictures of this alien's species. "He was alive after the crash. Maybe there are others, still alive, I mean."

"Maybe." Peters studied the corpse. "I don't see any external injuries, except for the blood around his mouth."

"He seems unarmed," Stonewall observed. "Maybe his species is friendly."

"Maybe. Let's see if we can get inside that ship."

Carefully, they climbed through the open exit door into the airlock. The inside door stood also open. The interior of the alien ship looked almost familiar. It didn't surprise Stonewall. Humanoid species tended to think alike.

They found another dead crewmember sitting in the co-pilot's chair. The other chair was empty. Stonewall assumed it had been occupied by the dead man outside.

The two creatures sitting in the passenger seats looked like giant slugs, dressed in leather. At first Stonewall thought they might be alive, but they didn't move when he approached. They hung limply in their harness, and their grotesque heads slumped forward.

A noise from the back of what looked like a storage room made both men swing around, their rifles aiming at the sound. As they tried to peer into the darkness of the room, a shadow appeared in the doorway, and a figure dressed in a loose blue uniform stumbled out. A humanoid male.

He looked different from the two dead men. His features were finely chiseled, almost feminine, his black hair cropped short. He could have passed for human, had it not been for the long, pointy ears and the purple eyes. The iris seemed to fill the entire socket. His uniform bulged strangely in his back, as if covering a backpack or a large hump.

One of his arms hung limply by his side, and there was blood on his chest. When he saw the two humans, he said something in an alien language neither understood.

"We are here to help you," Peters said. "Can you understand us?"

The man listened to his words and stood silent for a moment, and then he said, "I understand. You are from Earth?"

Peters nodded. "We are. We have an outpost here on this planet. Where are you from?"

"We come from far away, but we've been to your planet." He looked at the dead man in the co-pilot's seat. "Is he dead?"

"Yes, he is."

"And the other one?" The alien spoke slowly, coughed. Blood trickled down his chin.

"The other one is dead also. So are the two in the passenger seats. I'm sorry."

The alien man chuckled. "Do not be sorry. I am happy. We were their prisoners. Slaves."

"We? There are others?" Stonewall asked.

The man nodded and pointed into the storage room. "In there. You must wake them." He stumbled as he walked into the room. Then he sat down into one of the seats fastened to one wall. "I am injured." He coughed again. His eyes seemed to cloud over for a moment. "You must save them," he said, "please, save them."

Stonewall started to walk toward the storage room, but Peters held him back. "Be careful, it could be a trap."

The alien man looked up at them, his eyes pleading. "No trap. We are not warriors."

Stonewall held his weapon at the ready as he walked into the other room. It took him a moment for his eyes to adjust to the low light. Four coffin-like boxes stood against one wall, one of them with an open lid. He walked closer and looked into the first one. In the darkness, he saw the outlines of a human body inside the box. Looking for a way to open the coffin, he found a lever on one side. When he turned it, the lid sprang open.

Staring into the open box, he saw that it was indeed a body. The face was alien; it looked slack, like that of a dead person.

He walked back into the other room. "I think they're dead," he said with a low voice.

"Not dead," the alien man said. "In suspension. Just open the caskets and wait. They will wake up. Please, do not harm them."

"We won't," Peters assured him. "Don't worry."

Stonewall went into the storage room again and opened the other two boxes. The aliens inside looked remarkably like the first one. As he watched the one he opened first, a sudden twitch moved across the slack face, and then suddenly the eyes flew open.

Sitting up, the alien stared at Stonewall.

"Don't be afraid," Stonewall said with a soothing voice, not knowing if he would be understood. "We are friends."

The dark lips formed a smile. "Friends," the alien repeated with a soft, female voice. She sat up, and then she carefully climbed out of the casket.

Movement in the other two caskets told Stonewall that all of the aliens were alive. He watched them sitting up and leave their sleeping places. All three wore clothing similar to those of the wounded man in the other room. Even though it was loose, he could see the outlines of breasts on their chests.

The first one stared at Stonewall and spoke, but of course, he didn't understand a word.

"I don't understand your language," he said.

"But I understand *you*." The alien looked at Stonewall. "I recognize your language. What happened? Who are you?"

"Your spaceship crashed. We are here to rescue you."

"We crashed?" The female lifted her head and looked into the fourth coffin. "What happened to Leer? Is he alive?"

"If you mean your male companion, yes, he is alive, but he is injured." Stonewall walked ahead of them into the room where Peters and the alien man waited anxiously. When the three females stepped out, the wounded man let out an audible sigh. One of the three went over to him and squatted in front of him. She spoke to him in a soft, low voice, and then she stood up and faced Peters and Stonewall.

"He needs help. He will die if he doesn't get medical attention fast."

Peters looked at Stonewall. "Do you have any medical training?"

Stonewall shook his head. "Just some first aid, basics, that's all. He needs more than that."

"This is just crazy. I've told the Chief many times we need more than a few scooters and a couple of rovers. We need vehicles that fly, not just crawl on the ground!" Peters stared at the darkening sky outside.

"I wondered about that myself," Stonewall said. "Why don't we have a small shuttle?"

"Too dangerous, apparently. Because of the giant reptiles controlling the sky." Peters laughed sarcastically. "As if traveling on the ground is so safe."

"So what can we do?"

"There is no room on the scooter for all of us, obviously. I could take him back to the outpost. Doc Flemming might be able to help him. You'd have to stay here with these three and wait for us to pick you up with the rover. If I leave now, I should make it before midnight."

"I thought traveling at night is too dangerous?"

"It is." Peters studied the alien man who sat in a crouched position in his seat, his breath coming in great gasps. "But this is an emergency. I know which way to go now. It will be easier."

"All right. If you think so. I'll stay here. We should be safe inside this vessel."

"You should be, but don't get careless. Now, help me getting him outside and to the scooter."

The alien man could barely stand. Stonewall and Peters helped him outside then they practically dragged him across the swamp until they reached the scooter. Before Peters left, he gave Stonewall a pack, which had been stored in the back of the sidecar.

"There is water and food inside. It should be enough for you until I come back." Peters lowered his voice. "Don't let down your guard. Those might be females, but we know nothing about their species. Keep your eyes open at all times and your rifle within easy reach. I'll contact the base and fill them in about the situation. Don't expect anyone to pick you up until tomorrow afternoon. That rover doesn't travel any faster than the scooters, perhaps even slower." He slapped Stonewall on the back. "Take care and stay safe, my friend."

Stonewall watched as Peters took off into the forest then he waded back to the alien vessel. The three females watched him anxiously when he climbed back into the ship.

"Thank you for helping us," one of them said. "I am Sheera. What shall we call you?"

"Stonewall, call me Stonewall." He looked at the other two. "You have names also?"

Both of them smiled. For the first time, he noticed their long incisors.

"I am called Pteer."

"And I am Seel."

Stonewall tried to remember their names and the faces that went with them. Even though at first glance they looked alike, he noticed differences between them, the most important ones the eyes. Sheera's eyes were purple, Pteer's brown and Seel had shiny, black eyes. Watching them closer, he also noticed that their faces seemed unable to show deep expressions, as if they were wearing masks. They looked almost unfinished. Coarse. Their naked skulls were large, bulging out in the back of their heads.

When Sheera turned away from him, he saw the hump on her back, and checking out the other two, he found they also had humps.

He shrugged. Just because they weren't very attractive, didn't mean they couldn't be amiable.

"Is there a reason you are wearing protection over your head and face?" Sheera asked.

"Yes, there is. We find it uncomfortably hot and humid on this planet," Stonewall explained, "but we can survive without the protection."

"Can you take it off?"

"Why?"

She shrugged. "We feel..." she hesitated, "...disturbed, uneasy."

"Explain."

"The *Snaar* kidnapped us when our ship landed on one of the planets they control. Their Enforcers cover their faces with masks, terrible looking masks, to intimidate. We are intimidated."

Stonewall undid the straps that held his helmet and removed it. The humid air and the alien scents hit him with full force, and he gasped for a moment. "I'm not sure if this is such a good idea," he said, taking shallow breaths.

Sheera smiled. "We breathe the same air as Humans, and we adapt. You will, too." She stepped closer and looked into his face. "You are handsome," she said.

He became aware of another scent and realized it was her fragrance. Finding it quite pleasant, he inhaled deeply, feeling suddenly apprehensive by her nearness. She laughed softly and stepped back. "You know nothing about my species, don't you?" she said.

He shook his head. "No. I have to admit I've never even heard of you."

"We know much about yours. Our ships have visited your planet many times in the past. We are having dealings with some of your colony planets. That is how we learned your language, should you be wondering."

"The question has occurred to me," he admitted.

"Our species has a talent for learning languages, among other things."

"Are you hungry?" he asked. "I am hungry and thirsty, and I'm going to have something to eat now. You are welcome to share my food with me." He looked at the dead co-pilot. "But first I will get rid of him and those two other passengers. Can one of you help me?"

Seel volunteered to give him a hand. They took the corpses outside, one by one. Stonewall looked around, noticed that the sun had disappeared from vision. It would be dark soon. "Should we bury them? What is your custom?" he asked.

She shrugged. "They do not belong to our species. One of them is a Snaar. Let the wild beasts have them."

"But not here," Stonewall protested. "I'm not comfortable having scavengers or even carnivores snooping around this ship. They might even decide to add us to their meal."

"Then we should carry them into the forest," Seel suggested.

They did. After that, they carried the other dead alien away from the vessel and had him join his companion.

It was getting dark fast, and they hurried to get back into the comparative safety of the small ship.

"I wonder if the power is still working," Stonewall mused, looking around. "We could use some light."

"We don't know much about the workings of mechanical things," Pteer said. "We have not been taught."

Stonewall produced a small hand-lamp and shone it over an unfamiliar-looking instrument panel. He gave up after a short time, not wanting to blow up the ship by pushing the wrong buttons. He shrugged. "I guess my light will have to do. As long as I can see what I'm eating."

Sheera got up and closed the exit door. "We don't want any unwanted visitors," she said.

Stonewall sat in one of the seats and rummaged inside his pack, found the food, and took it out. He also found a number of bottles filled with water. He handed one to the girls. "Here, you'll have to share it, because I don't have that many." Then he offered them each a sandwich. "I hope you can eat my food."

Seel smelled her sandwich and then she took a bite. Munching on it, she said, "We are not much different, your species and mine. Our metabolism is similar. We can eat your food without ill effects. Most of it, anyway."

Stonewall felt a slight breeze coming from a crack in the ceiling. It felt refreshing. When he looked up, he could see a narrow strip of the dark sky, dotted with stars. "I hope it doesn't start raining," he said, wondering if there were animals out there that could use this entrance to the ship to check out the interior.

Though tired, he felt uneasy about going to sleep. After all, he didn't know anything about his companions and he remembered Peters' warning, but he finally surrendered to his body's demands.

[5]

HE AWOKE WHEN SOMEONE TOUCHED HIM ON THE SHOULDER. Opening his eyes, it took a moment for him to orient himself. A figure crouched in front of him. Looking into a pair of purple eyes, he remembered and sat up straight. "What is it, Sheera?"

The alien female put a finger against her lips. "There is someone outside," she whispered.

"Who?" he whispered back. Looking up, he saw a streak of light through the crack in the ceiling. "How long did I sleep?"

She smiled faintly. "It is morning. You must have been tired."

Listening, he heard noises outside. Scrabbling noises. He realized someone, or something was climbing onto the ship. Still looking up, he suddenly saw a shadow blocking the crack in the ceiling and then a pair of faceted eyes, like the eyes of a giant fly, staring down at them.

Bugeyes!

"I think we have company," he said. "Unfortunately, not the company I expected."

Sheera followed his gaze and let out a little shriek.

A loud noise inside the airlock and then someone pulled open the door. Stonewall jumped up and grabbed the inside lever to close it again, but his strength didn't match the creature who pulled on the other side.

He stepped back, reached for his rifle, but decided it wouldn't do any good, remembering Peters telling him about the orders not to shoot.

The creature that stepped through the open door stood about five feet tall. It looked remarkably like a giant ant. Looking around with its faceted eyes, it moved further into the room and began to herd Stonewall and the three females toward the exit door.

Stonewall looked outside and saw a few of the *Bugeyes* waiting in the tall grass. Shrugging, he let himself be pushed out of the door.

"They are going to take us with them," Sheera said beside him.

He glanced at her. "How do you know?"

"I can hear them inside my head. They speak only with their minds."

"You can read thoughts?"

She shook her head. "Not really. This is different. They broadcast their thoughts like radio waves. That's how they communicate with each other. I can hear them."

"Can you talk to them?"

"I think so."

"Ask them what they want from us."

She stood silent for a moment, and then she shrugged. "They are ignoring me."

"Maybe they can't hear you."

"They can, but they don't want to talk to me."

"Damn!" Stonewall cursed, remembering his protective helmet. His only connection to the base lay inside the alien ship. Nobody would know about their capture by the giant insects.

He looked around and saw a great number of the *Bugeyes* milling around. Some of them seemed interested in them, but they soon turned away and began lining up in rows, almost like a troop of soldiers. He saw a few of the giant bugs carrying long boxes out of the alien ship. They strapped them on the backs of some of their larger members.

He wondered what the boxes contained.

A small group surrounded the captives, and they began moving in a solid group, away from the stranded vessel.

Stonewall, being taller than the Ants, looked ahead and saw a few of them leading the column, like scouts. Twisting his head, he saw the same thing in the rear.

These guys are intelligent. They are soldiers returning from some task.

He didn't see any weapons, but looking at their mandibles, he didn't see any need for weapons. They could cut a Human in half should they decide to become hostile.

He also noticed that what Peters called *Ants* only appeared to look like ants. They walked upright on two thin, but strong legs. They had two long arms and two short, rudimentary appendages. From their large, oval heads sprouted two thin antennas, which were in constant motion.

A small abdomen hung below a broad thorax. They didn't appear to wear any clothing.

"Can you still hear them talking to each other?" he asked Sheera, who walked beside him.

She shook her head. "They are silent. Only once in a while one of them sends out a signal. And I don't understand what they are saying. They sound almost like direction-signals."

Even though it was still early in the day, the sun already shone hot down upon them, and the humidity seemed unchanged. Stonewall breathed in the hot and humid air, aware of the overpowering reek of decaying vegetation, mainly fungus. He became also aware of all sizes of insects buzzing around them.

"It is hot," one of the other two females complained. "This is not a friendly planet."

Stonewall chuckled. "I don't know what kind of environment you are used to, but for me, this is hell. I've been here only three days, and it seems like an eternity. So far, I have nothing good to report, should I survive this ordeal."

"What are your people doing on this planet?" Sheera asked.

"We are observers," Stonewall said.

"Observers of what?"

He shrugged. "Of space."

"You observe space?"

"That's right. That's how we discovered your arrival here. Aren't you lucky?"

She laughed. "Very. Look what is happening to us."

"Let me ask you a question. Why are you here?"

"We crashed."

When he glanced at her, he saw her smile. "I know you did. But what is your reason for being here in this sector of space?"

"We have no reason for being here. This planetary system is unknown to us. The last thing I remember is sitting inside a place where you eat, on a planet we meant to trade with, when three *Snaar*-Enforcers approached our table and told us to come with them. I don't remember how we ended up in those Suspension-units of the *Snaar*-spaceship."

"You were kidnapped. Where were they intending to take you?"

"Probably to one of their planets where slavery is legal."

"What did they want with you?"

She threw him a quick look. "You are ignorant of our species, otherwise you wouldn't ask. Females of my species are quite popular with certain males and some females. I cannot tell you any more."

Laughing grimly, he said, "You don't have to. I can guess the reason."

"No, you can't, but you may have the opportunity to find out."

She stayed silent after that. Stonewall grew weary. The *Bugeyes* moved quickly, and he found it difficult after a while to keep up the pace, not being used to walking long distances.

"How are you doing?" he asked Sheera, when she suddenly stumbled.

"I am getting fatigued," she said. "My sisters and I are nearing the end of our juvenile cycle. We are approaching adulthood."

"You are not adults of your species?"

"We will soon be."

Stonewall mulled over what Sheera told him. These were girl-children of a species he never heard of before coming here. Suddenly, considering himself a babysitter, he felt a heavy weight settling upon his shoulders. Children needed to be protected, since most could not defend themselves as easily as an adult could, lacking experience and judgment of dangerous situations.

He was a trained scout, capable of just that sort of thing. He needed to be strong.

He would not fail them.

Once, the walking column stopped and drew together into a tight knot of chitinous bodies. Hearing a noise, like the flapping of great wings, Stonewall looked up and saw the dark silhouette of one of the flying dragons against the clouds. Too close for comfort, he decided.

It circled for a while, but then it moved on.

The second time they stopped occurred for a completely different reason.

A large animal, it looked like a cross between a rhinoceros, a giraffe and a spider, crossed their path. Everything happened with such incredible speed, Stonewall could hardly follow the event.

About half the group of soldiers swarmed around the unfortunate animal and attacked it, giving it barely time for just one cut-off strangled scream before it collapsed on the ground.

Then the soldiers, hunters now in Stonewall's mind, began cutting the huge carcass into small pieces.

"I think I figured out what our new friends were doing out here," Stonewall said.

"Hunting," Sheera said. "Fortunately, they didn't consider us food."

"They still might. We could be either the appetizer or the dessert."

When the group moved again, most of the *Bugeyes* were loaded down with large chunks of meat, which they carried in their mandibles.

Stonewall shuddered, trying not to think about what would have happened had the *Bugeyes* decided to add him and his companions to their daily quota. He could only imagine the strength these giant insects possessed. Witnessing the speed they displayed bringing down their victim, he had no illusions about his own possible fate. Not even his flash-rifle would have saved him.

Even so, he would have felt better having that rifle with him. It would have given him at least some small measure of security, as false as it probably would have been.

He wondered if Peters made if safely back to the outpost and if they sent out a rover to pick up him and the alien girls, wondered also if they'd sent out a rescue-team when they discovered them missing.

By late afternoon, he was exhausted, thirsty and hungry. He missed his pack and the food and water it contained.

They had left the swamp behind a long time ago and traveled most of the time through a dense forest of mushrooms and fern-like vegetation. The forest ended suddenly, and they traveled across a barren, sandy land. Their destination seemed to be a tall, cone-shaped structure rising from the hard ground some distance away.

His assumption turned out to be correct. They arrived at the foot of the mound a couple of hours later, shortly before sundown.

The mound reminded Stonewall of a giant termite hill. Dark holes at regular intervals dotted the smooth, hard surface. Stonewall didn't know if they were vents, windows, or places allowing entry into the huge structure.

A giant opening, guarded by sentries, turned out to be their destination.

Stonewall expected to be walking in darkness, but to his surprise, he found the wide tunnel they entered almost as bright as outside. When he looked for the source of the light, he saw thousands of light-bugs crawling on the ceiling and along the smooth walls. The cooler temperature and the lower humidity inside the *Hive* also surprised him pleasantly.

The road they traveled led upward in a tight spiral. As the procession of *Bugeyes* made its way to the top, small groups disappeared into secondary tunnels.

Stonewall became certain that they must be close to the top when the small group that still accompanied them stopped.

The tunnel had widened into a large cavern. A number of smaller tunnels led away from the main one. A group of *Bugeyes* came out of one of these tunnels. They were smaller and slimmer than the ones who captured him and the females. They approached and stood rigid in front of them, regarding him and the girls silently, only their antennas moved.

"What are they saying?" he asked Sheera.

"They want to know what manner of creature I and my sisters are. They seem to be familiar with your species."

"Can you talk to these?"

"I'll try." She became silent. After a short time, she said, "They told me not to resist, and we won't be harmed. We are supposed to come with them."

"I don't think we have much of a choice," Stonewall said, chuckling as if he had told a joke. Besides feeling tired, he was also dirty and uncomfortable. His clothing seemed to be glued against his body, and he wanted to submerge himself in a tub of cold water. After that, a juicy steak and a glass of chilled fruit juice would just about take him to nirvana.

The embrace of a passionate woman would also be appreciated.

He followed the new group of *Bugeyes*. Sheera walked close beside him. Her hand reached for his. "I am afraid," she whispered. Her sisters Seel and Pteer walked on his other side. Both of them had not said much during their ordeal. Sheera seemed to do most of the talking.

When he looked at the girl to his left and saw her glance at him with her black eyes, he knew it was Seel. She also put her hand into his. He felt her shiver. "Don't be scared," he tried to reassure them, not feeling too brave himself. For all he knew they might be slaughtered.

They walked down a narrow tunnel and then turned into another one. It ended in a large room. Stonewall saw the darkening sky through an opening in one wall and knew that they were inside one of the rooms on the outside of the structure.

He also saw furniture in the room. Nothing remotely like what Humans would build but definitely recognizable as furniture.

On a chair-like contraption sat a giant Ant, much larger than any of the others he'd seen so far. Beside it, on benches, sat a group of smaller *Bugeyes*, most of them also quite large. The creature on the chair watched them. Its glittering multifaceted eyes seemed to regard them with interest. It could have been nothing more but the interest a carnivore shows its intended meal.

What are you doing on our world?

The words sounded clear and audible inside Stonewall's head. He knew with certainty that the giant Ant had not spoken aloud. He stood rigid and stared at the creature.

A silent sound, almost like laughter, made him doubt his sanity. This giant insect could not possibly communicate directly with him. He must be imagining it.

Sheer stirred beside him. "Our vessel crashed," she said.

So the hunters have reported. You came from the sky in a giant egg. I

31

am addressing the other one, the male. His species has been on our world for many seasons.

"I have been here only for a short time," Stonewall protested.

Do not lie. I have seen many of you spying on my workforce and my hunters. What is your purpose here?

"We are using your world as a base to watch our enemies. Those who want to harm my species." It was not a lie but not quite the whole truth. "May I ask what your position is in this city of yours?"

I am the Queen.

How do you address the queen of a bunch of giant bugs? They had not taught him to deal with a situation like this one. "What are you planning to do with us, your Majesty?" he asked, hoping he used the correct intonation.

We will observe you, so we can determine if you represent danger. You are an unknown element on our world.

"We did not come here to harm your people or your world. You will find that we are peaceful." What an outright lie! Stonewall almost choked on the words. Humans and peace were on opposite sides. Earth had never seen peace. Ever.

I hope so, for your sake.

The queen rose from her chair. She towered above Stonewall as she came closer, a frightening and imposing creature. He didn't flinch when she reached out to touch him on the chest with one of her hands. Bony fingers dug into his ribs.

You are soft on the outside, she said.

"Yes, we are. Our bodies are different from yours and easily damaged," he said, trying not to scream from the pain her touch produced and took an involuntary step backward.

Your companions are not like you, she observed.

"But we can also be damaged," Sheera said.

The Queen took away her hand and Stonewall breathed a sigh of relief. One of the *Bugeyes* who had brought them gave Stonewall a gentle push. He followed the two that walked ahead of him.

They entered a tunnel and walked down a short distance. Stopping in front of an opening, the creature pushed Stonewall through it. Inside a small room, he looked around and saw a thick blanket of some soft material on the floor, obviously a bed. He turned when he heard someone else coming into the room.

Recognizing Sheera in the semi-darkness, he was happy to see her and her sisters. At least he wouldn't be alone.

Sheera came close and leaned against him. Pteer and Seel stumbled over to the bed and slumped onto it.

"I am so tired," Sheera said with a low voice. "Come, lie beside me and hold me."

Her body felt soft and warm as she lay in his arms, but he was too tired to think about it. He fell asleep almost immediately.

[6]

WHEN HE OPENED HIS EYES AGAIN, SHEERA STILL LAY IN HIS embrace. He didn't know how long he'd slept. For all he knew, it could be the next day or still the same evening.

In the dim light of the light-bugs, he saw Pteer and Seel lying on either side of him. All three of the girls were still asleep.

He disengaged himself from Sheera and without waking the girls, carefully rose to his feet. Surprised to see the opening to their room unguarded, he stepped into the tunnel.

Seeing nobody, he began walking slowly down the narrow tunnel, but first he scratched a mark into the wall near the opening with his pocketknife. The round holes in the smooth wall of the tunnel all looked alike; one could easily get lost.

He peered into the different rooms, but all of them were empty until, further down, he heard voices from one of the rooms. Human voices.

Curious and excited, he almost ran to investigate the source of the voices, but before he reached it, a figure stepped out into the tunnel. A man. There was no question about it.

The man saw him the same time he did and froze. Then he let out a surprised shout and came running toward Stonewall, grabbing him by the shoulder. "I don't know who you are," the man shouted, "but you feel real to me, and you are a welcome sight. Did you come to rescue us?"

Stonewall shook his head, too stunned to speak. "I'm a prisoner, just as you obviously are. You must be either Maisoneuve or Wong."

The man let go of him, disappointment clearly visible on his haggard, unshaven face. Stepping back, he said, "I'm Maisoneuve. Who are you?"

"I'm the new guy, Terrex Stonewall." He gave Maisoneuve a tight smile. Even through the stubble, he could tell that the man was older than most of the scouts on the base. In his early thirties, at least. "They figured you dead. I'm glad to see you alive. It means there is hope yet, but don't expect any rescue. We're on our own."

"Fuck it!" Maisoneuve cursed and pulled Stonewall into the room. "Come inside, they don't like it if we walk around freely." He gave a dry laugh. "As if we could escape. Not without wings anyway."

The other man inside the room stared at Stonewall for a moment, and then he chuckled. "For a moment there, I thought I was still dreaming," he said, "but I guess you're real. Not everything you see around here is real, you know."

"I don't understand."

"The *Bugs* like to play mind games with us," Maisoneuve explained. "Be on guard. Don't believe everything you see and hear." He stepped back suddenly and stared at Stonewall. "How do I know you're not just one of their tricks?"

Stonewall laughed. "How do I know you're not?"

"How did you get here?" Wong asked.

"The Chief sent Peters and me to investigate the alien ship and, hopefully, find you two," Stonewall explained.

"Is Peters here also?"

"No, he went back to the station with one of the injured aliens. He left me behind with three of the survivors, but before Peters could come back to pick us up, we were captured by the *Bugeyes*. That's all I can tell you."

"You must have arrived after we left to investigate the crashed ship." Maisoneuve gave Stonewall a look filled with pity. "You unlucky bastard. Not a good way to start your new assignment. You said there were survivors. Are they with you?"

"Yes, they are. Three females."

"Females? Pretty?"

Stonewall shrugged. "They are aliens. Their concept of beauty may be different from ours."

"Ugly then, huh? Are they at least humanoid?" Wong asked.

"Yes, they are humanoid. I'd better get back before they wake up and find me gone. They might wonder what happened and start panicking. Why don't you come with me, so you can meet them? Or better yet, why don't you move in with us?"

He turned and stepped into the tunnel. Not waiting for the two men to join him, he started walking back to the room with the girls.

One of them, Seel, stirred and sat up when the men entered the room. She saw them and poked her sisters, saying something in her language, and then she rose from the bed. Recognizing Stonewall, she relaxed visibly and asked, "Are these your people? Have they come to rescue us?"

He shook his head and smiled faintly. "These are my people, but they haven't come to rescue us. They are prisoners, just like us. Their names are Wong and Maisoneuve." He turned to the two men and said, "This is Seel. The other two are Sheera and Pteer."

The girls on the bed stood and came closer. Sheera touched Stonewall's arm and leaned against him. "I worried when I saw you gone, Stonewall," she whispered. "Please, don't leave us."

"Don't worry, I won't," he said soothingly and put his arm around her waist. "I'm sorry if I gave you cause to be concerned." He didn't miss the look Maisoneuve threw Wong.

"How long have you known these...these ladies?" Maisoneuve asked, lifting his brows.

"A couple of days now. Why?"

"Well...you seem to be quite chummy with them."

Stonewall laughed, color creeping into his face. "It's not what it looks like. I just feel I have to protect them." He took away his arm from Sheera's waist.

"Protect them?" Maisoneuve pulled Stonewall aside. "My God, Stonewall," he whispered. "Have you looked at them? I mean *really* looked? They're not exactly beauty-queen material. In fact, they're downright ugly."

"They're not that ugly," Stonewall protested.

Maisoneuve gave him a quizzing look. "Are you really that hard-up for pussy? You don't even know if they have a vagina."

"If you're referring to our sex-organs, let me assure you, we have one."

Stonewall turned and looked at Sheera, who stood staring at them. "I apologize for his remark," he said lamely.

She favored him with a bright smile and stepped up to him. Looking into his eyes, she said, "You don't have to apologize for him," and lifted up to give him a quick kiss.

Maisoneuve laughed beside him. "Not only has she good hearing, she's also got you wrapped around her little finger...if she has one."

"She has one," Stonewall said, annoyed. "You're wrong about my relationship with these girls. There is nothing sexual here."

"I didn't mean to offend you," Maisoneuve said. "We want you to be aware that you may be the target of a plot."

"A plot? By whom?"

"The *Bugeyes*. When did you say you arrived here?"

"Yesterday."

"These three were with you?"

"Of course they were." Stonewall shook his head. "What's this about?"

"They might be screwing with your mind. Watch yourself." Maisoneuve scratched his beard and looked at Wong. "I think we'd better get back to our room. The *Bugs* don't like us wandering around. Besides, they'll be bringing our breakfast soon. Don't want to miss that."

Before they walked out, Maisoneuve turned and said, "Be on guard, Stonewall. How do you know we were here? Think about that."

"What did he mean?" Sheera asked.

Stonewall shrugged. "I have no idea. He sounded very confused."

"I am thirsty and hungry," Seel said. "That man Maisoneuve mentioned food."

A shadow darkened the door, and one of their captors stepped into the room. It carried a tray woven from reeds. On the tray stood four bowls and a pitcher. Setting the tray on the floor, it looked at Sheera then it turned and departed.

"Food and water," Sheera said. "It told me to take the nourishment. It will not harm us."

Stonewall squatted and picked up one of the bowls. He dipped his finger into the green jelly-like substance inside and tasted it. "Not much taste," he said. "A little too sweet, reminds me of honey." He looked at Sheera. "What do you think? Is it safe to eat it?"

"Your friends seemed to think so." She shrugged. "We have to eat something." Then she scooped out a gob with two fingers and put it into her mouth. After swallowing it, she laughed. "Doesn't taste much different from the fare they serve on *Fargass*."

Stonewall took a swig from the pitcher. "Water," he said. "I hope I don't get sick from it. I've been inoculated against all kinds of diseases, but then you never know what kind of critters live in the local waters."

They finished their meals, and Stonewall had to admit, his spirits lifted, having filled his stomach, and quenched his thirst. The girls seemed to share his feeling of well-being. He remembered his grandfather, a beekeeper, telling him that honey was the best food there was. According to him, it prolonged life. Maybe it was true; after all, he lived to be one hundred and five years old. But that could also have been due to the elimination of many diseases Humans died of.

Almost as if someone were watching them, as soon as they finished with their food, one of the *Bugeyes* came to pick up the tray with the empty bowls. A few moments later, two more of them came in. One of them addressed Sheera.

"They want me to go with them," she told the others.

"Are you sure it's wise?" Stonewall asked.

"I don't receive any menacing emanations from them."

The two creatures left the room. Sheera followed them.

Stonewall sat on the soft bed, since it was the only piece of furniture in the room. Crossing their legs, Seel and Pteer sat down beside him. "What is your relationship to that male who was in the fourth casket?" he asked the girl.

"Leer? He is our protector. It is his job to make our transition into adulthood easier." Seel looked at him out of black eyes. "Since he is not here, and he may not have survived his injuries, are you willing to replace him?"

"I don't understand."

"When we change, certain activities need to be performed to complete our transition. Are you willing to help us?" Her eyes glittered in the semidarkness like two dark pools of water, reflecting the light of the stars in the night sky. He realized the tiny bright spots in her black eyes were the crawling light-bugs on the ceiling.

"What is expected of me?" he asked.

She smiled. "We will let you know. As long as we can count on you."

He laid his hand on hers. "I'll do anything to help you. I'm your friend." He felt the heat from her body flowing into his arm, and he wondered why she felt so hot. A tingling in his groin made him pull his hand away, and he hoped she wouldn't notice his sudden discomfort.

She smiled happily. "My time is near. I think I'll be the first one." She bent forward and kissed him on the mouth. "Thank you," she whispered. Looking at Pteer, who lay on the bed asleep, she said, "I will join my sister and rest. I feel very tired."

"I hope you're not ill," Stonewall said, concerned about her welfare.

"Oh, no. I am fine. This is what happens when our time comes." She stretched out beside Pteer and closed her eyes.

Stonewall got up from the bed and walked to the door, wondering about Seel's remark and worried about Sheera. He didn't know if he should go visit Maisoneuve and Wong, but, looking at the sleeping girls, decided against it.

Sheera came back before lunch. Her demeanor seemed normal but Stonewall had the distinct feeling that something had happened to her. "Are you all right?" he asked.

She nodded and smiled. "I am fine."

"What did they do to you?"

"I talked with the Queen. She wanted to know about my species and asked about yours. I told her as much as I knew. Then they took samples of my blood and examined me." She looked preoccupied. "They are not as primitive as we thought at first. They are quite intelligent and possess great knowledge."

"They use tools and make pottery," Stonewall mused. "That tray woven from reeds displayed skill and creative thought."

They didn't get anything to eat for lunch. Stonewall didn't feel hungry anyway. Sheera lay down beside her sisters and fell into a deep slumber.

Two *Bugeyes* came shortly after noon. This time they spoke to Stonewall. He could hear them clearly inside his head.

Come with us. As if reading his thoughts, the creature said, *Your companions will be safe.*

He followed them reluctantly.

They walked down the tunnel they had come through the night before. Then they turned into another side-tunnel. It ended in a large room with a high ceiling. Stonewall suppressed a shout of surprise when he entered the room.

He had stepped into a garden. A pool in the middle held clear water that came bubbling out of a hole in the wall. Softly glowing shrubs grew from the ground, which was covered by a carpet of soft moss-like vegetation.

The water is refreshing and cleansing. The Queen wants you to cleanse your body.

They turned and left him standing alone. He walked into the room, toward the pool, bent down and put his hand into the water. It could be acid, as far as he knew. He didn't trust these giant bugs. The water felt cool but not cold. He pulled the boots from his aching feet, and then he undressed. Naked, he stepped into the cool water, and slowly, he sank into the welcoming liquid. Immersing his whole body, he lay there, relaxed and with his eyes closed. Well, this was more like it. Life was great.

The sound of soft footsteps had him opening his eyes. He sat up with a start when he saw the figure walking towards him.

"No," he yelled, "that is not possible. You can't be here."

"Hello, Terrex," she said with her soft voice, opening her robe.

[7]

HE STARED AT HER NAKED WHITE BODY. SHE WAS AS BEAUTIFUL as he remembered. A little full in the hips and heavy of thigh, but her breasts were firm and stood out proudly displaying her thick pink nipples.

She turned slightly and presented her buttocks. She knew he'd always loved her buttocks. Fleshy and round, they turned him on immensely.

She made that silly giggling sound when she knew that he wanted to make love to her. "You haven't changed, have you, Terrex? Still as horny as ever."

He rubbed his eyes. "You can't be here, Lucinda. This place is light-years away from Earth. How did you get here?"

"I flew in a ship. How else, Silly?" She squatted on the edge of the pool.

"But how did you get in here? I mean, this is a colony of huge ants. Are you a prisoner like me?" He felt his penis rising as he stared at her pink clit, peeking at him from between her slightly spread thighs.

She was right. He was horny. Extremely horny, and he wanted nothing more than to grab her, throw her onto the soft ground and plunge his hurting cock into her tight pussy.

Again, she smiled at him and reached out to touch his cheek. "I know what you want, Love. I want that also. Come out and make love to me."

"You haven't answered my question. Are you a prisoner?"

"No, of course not. Now, are you coming out, or do I have to come in?"

He sighed. "How about you coming in?"

She put her feet at the edge of the pool and slid into the water, giggling wickedly. "Are you trying to be difficult?" she asked.

Slithering up to him, she ducked her head under water and put her lips onto his stiff mast. Then she sucked it into her mouth.

He groaned, closing his eyes. There could be no doubt; this was Lucinda, the love of his life. The one who caused him to leave Earth to come to this place. The same Lucinda who cheated on him with her cousin. She loved to fuck, and she loved to give head. And she was good at both.

Coming up for air, she turned and slid on top of him, her breasts grazing his chest. "You always liked when I did that to you, didn't you?"

"You know I did. Still do." He took her face between his hands. Her lips opened when he kissed her fiercely. She sucked on his tongue, gently pressing her teeth into the soft tissue.

Her hand snaked between them, her fingers curled around his penis, forming a soft sheath. Moving her hand up and down, she laughed into his mouth when he pulled away.

"Don't make me come like that," he breathed, separating his mouth from hers.

She laughed softly. "You used to like it when I jerked you off."

"That was before I experienced what you can do with your pussy," he said, grinning.

"Well...I'm offering it to you." She put her warm lips against his. "Why are you hesitating?"

"Not in the water."

"All right." She rose and bent forward, presenting her ample buttocks. Looking back at him over her shoulder, she said, "How's this?"

He stared at her hairless pussy-lips peeking at him from between her fleshy cheeks. She wriggled her bottom. "Come on. What are you waiting for?"

Groaning, he came out of the water, moved behind her, and put his rigid pole between her soft cheeks. She lifted up on tiptoes and captured his penis between her strong thighs. Moving her hips, she rubbed her clit over his straining member.

"That feels good," he said. Taking hold of his hard mast, he put it partially into her slippery vagina.

"Shove that big cock of yours already into me," she moaned and pushed back, grabbing his penis with her thick labia.

His hands clamped around her hips and, with a forceful thrust, he penetrated her, sliding easily into the creamy interior of her sweet cunt. A loud moan of pleasure escaped his lips, and he began hammering behind her like a man gone berserk.

"There is no hurry, Love," she moaned. "We have all the time in the world."

His head swam in a sea of pleasure as he moved slowly in and out of her hot sheath. "I've missed this," he groaned. "I've missed this so much. I've missed you."

"I'm here now." She squeezed his throbbing penis. "Just make love to me."

He lost all sense of time, just moved behind her, slamming his taut belly into her soft buttocks with a steady rhythm, unaware of his surroundings.

When he finally climaxed, it came with a rush so strong, he couldn't keep from shouting for joy.

Lucinda milked him until he grew limp inside her then she pulled away and sank to her knees. Turning lazily onto her back, she sank beneath the water, leaving only her face above the surface. "That was wonderful," she said and smiled up at him.

Raising her leg, she used her toes to play with his limp penis and giggled. "Looks like I sucked him dry."

He knelt beside her in the water. Pulling her up, he hugged her to him. "I don't know how you got here, but I'm happy you came. Let's dry off and relax. I need to hold you for a while."

A sudden slight breeze felt cool on his naked skin. He used his shirt to dry himself, and then he rubbed down Lucinda's voluptuous body. Afterwards, they lay on the soft moss, wrapped in each other's arms.

Feeling drowsy and content, he closed his eyes.

When he awoke, he was alone.

He sat up, looked around if he could see her anywhere. Then he called, "Lucinda?" without getting an answer. It seemed eerily silent in the garden; the only sound the gentle splashing of water filling the pool.

Sniffing the air, he found it laden with a sweet scent, like honey and lavender. He rose to his feet and looked for his clothing, found it in a heap beside the pool. When he picked up his shirt, it felt wet.

He knew he had taken a bath, but instead of feeling refreshed, his body seemed tired, exhausted.

Wonder what happened to Lucinda? Was she really here, or did I imagine her?

He looked down at his penis. It appeared chafed.

I fucked someone, but if it wasn't Lucinda, who? Certainly not one of those giant ants.

Deep in thought, he dressed. His shirt felt uncomfortably wet on his skin. He remembered Maisoneuve's words. *They might be screwing with your mind.*

Maybe they were, but not with just his mind!

The girls seemed upset when he came back into the room, but also relieved to see him unharmed. Sheera came into his arms. Looking up at him, she said, "I worried. Are you all right?"

"I'm fine."

"What did they do to you?"

"Nothing. I took a bath." He chuckled, grimly. "You may be right. These creatures are not as primitive as they appear."

A scraping sound from the door made him turn. One of the giant ants came walking in, carrying a tray. Putting it on the floor, it left again.

"I am actually quite hungry," Stonewall said.

Aside from the pitcher of water, the tray held a large bowl filled with some kind of fruit. The fruit reminded him of cherries and papayas. Having had no ill effects after consuming breakfast, he took a bite out of one of the larger fruit. "They're good," he said around a mouthful. "You girls should eat."

After they ate, Stonewall said, "I'm going to visit the two men. You'll be okay without me?"

The girls nodded but seemed reluctant to see him leave them again.

Maisoneuve and Wong lay on their beds when he entered their room. Both men sat up when they saw him.

"I have to talk with you about something," Stonewall said. "They took me into a garden. There I saw my ex-girlfriend. She couldn't be here. Tell me what happened to me?"

The two men chuckled.

"Did you have sex?" Wong asked.

Stonewall nodded. "I believe I did."

"Be assured, you did. Wong and I have a theory. They can manipulate time and space. Make things happen."

"Are you telling me it was my ex-girlfriend I had sex with? You're saying she was actually here? In the flesh?"

"I'm saying nothing. What is reality? May she was...maybe she wasn't." He lifted his shoulders. "Who knows?"

"You're talking nonsense, Maisoneuve." Stonewall stared at the other man. "Did you have a similar experience?"

"I did, and so did Wong. Actually, I'm planning to go the garden tomorrow morning." Maisoneuve grinned. "Let's face it, we haven't had a chance to screw a woman ever since we came to Epsilon. You may have noticed...there are no women on the station."

"You're outta luck here, unless you like Tommy better than his cooking," Wong snickered beside him.

Stonewall shook his head and left.

Manipulating time and space, indeed! Someone obviously had messed with the minds of those two men.

The sound of boots on the hard floor of the tunnel made him stop and look back. Wong caught up with him and shook his arm. "Listen, be careful. Don't let them stick any needles into you or anything like that. They did that to Maisoneuve and look how he's talking and behaving now. I think he's going crazy."

"And you?" Stonewall gave him an inquiring look.

"I'm fine, man. I never had sex with no one. I'm just pretending in front of Maisoneuve." He pulled on Stonewall's arm. "Come, I want to show you something."

Stonewall walked beside him toward the tavern-like room. Wong took him into one of the side-tunnels. It ended in another large room. They didn't see anyone, so they walked into it.

"Strange," Stonewall commented. "There are no guards. There isn't anyone around anywhere. We could probably escape."

The waning light of evening shone through an opening in one wall.

Wong chuckled. "Go, take a look." He gave Stonewall an encouraging shove.

Stepping carefully up to the big hole, Stonewall peered outside. The hard ground of the desert lay far below them. He hadn't realized that they were this. In the distance, he saw the umbrellas of a mushroom forest.

"We're pretty much at the top of this structure," Wong said beside him. "They don't need to post any guards. There is no way out of here, unless you can grow a pair of wings."

"How about just walking down the road we came?"

"Forget it." Wong shook his head. "We tried the first day we came here. They do have guards two floors down. Nobody gets past them, not even the other ants. It seems the upper floors are reserved for the aristocracy. You may have noticed. They do look a little different."

"I noticed."

"Maisoneuve, in his lucid moments, has a theory about that also. He thinks they're a different species."

"It's possible. It is not unusual for two different species to live together. These up here could be parasitic and be living off the labor of the ants below. They seem to be smarter than the ones who caught us." Stonewall mused.

Wong chuckled. "There are plenty of Humans who let other people do their work for them. It doesn't mean they are necessarily smarter. They're just more ruthless. Or maybe they were born rich. That doesn't make them a different species."

"I guess not." Stonewall moved away from the opening. "Too bad we don't have any way of communicating with the station. If they knew our whereabouts I'm sure the Chief would send out a rescue team."

"He would, but we have no way of letting them know where we are." Wong cursed under his breath. "You know, if the Union of Scouts would get decent funding, we'd be better equipped. We'd have at least one flyer and maybe a couple of armored ground vehicles. With one of those, we could just drive into this place, without any problems."

"A small platoon of trained soldiers would also help," Stonewall suggested. "The *Bugeyes* wouldn't stand a chance."

"Well, we have neither. Let's face it, Stonewall, we are fucked." Wong sounded bitter. "I was only supposed to be here for one year. This is my third. Apparently, there wasn't another mission closer to home. How long did you sign on for?"

"One year."

Wong let out a dry laugh. "Don't count on that. But then again, we may never get out of here alive. So it doesn't really matter, does it?"

"We'll get out. I'm not giving up hope. They haven't harmed us yet. We're just assuming that they are hostile."

"Glad you're thinking positive. That's good. Now, let's get out of here."

Stonewall had difficulty falling asleep that night, even though the number of light-bugs seemed to have decreased, leaving the room much darker than during the day. Nightmares kept awaking him, but he finally managed to sink into an uneasy slumber.

He awoke to the soft touch of someone's hand on his chest.

[8]

Seeing a shadow hovering above him, he asked, "What is it?" He kept his voice barely above a whisper.

"You said you would assist us," a female voice whispered back.

"Assist in what?"

"Our transition."

"Your transition? Oh, right, I remember. Is that you, Seel?"

"Yes, and I am asking you for your help, as you promised."

"What is it you want me to do?"

She kissed him. He felt some of her saliva trickle into his mouth, found its taste pleasant and sweet. When he inhaled, he noticed the strong scent of her body. It intoxicated him.

"Don't fight it, please." She began tugging on his pants. "Take off your clothing," she whispered.

A sudden throbbing in his loin and his penis growing thick inside the confines of his pants, easily convinced him to strip. She didn't wait until he took off his shirt. He became aware of her nudity when she straddled him and began rubbing her pubes over his hard pole.

His eyes had adjusted to the darkness. Watching her silhouette swaying above him, he saw the outlines of her breasts. Reaching up, he put his hands around her narrow waist. Her skin felt warm and smooth.

"Be patient," she whispered. "I need to adjust myself to you."

Her vagina-lips molded themselves around the thick head of his penis. She kept rubbing her clit back and forth. When warm liquid dripped onto his thighs, she lifted her lower body. His hard cock snapped up and entered her cunt. She seemed terribly tight at first, but then she opened up, and he slid easily into her clutching sheath.

"Aaahh," he groaned, trying not to let out a loud shout of elation.

She writhed above him with slow movements. He wanted to explode inside the warm comfort of her tight organ but held back, enjoying the unbelievable pleasure. Even coupling with Lucinda had never been this intense. Maybe it was the thought that the female he fucked wasn't human but alien, or maybe he was just extremely horny. It didn't matter. He didn't want it to end.

He heard soft mewling sounds escaping her mouth as she suddenly sat still, trembling above him. Inside her vagina, her muscles pulsed around his throbbing shaft, squeezing it forcefully.

Letting out a loud hiss, she relaxed and began moving again.

"Do not hurry with your own release," she whispered, "I need you to be inside me as long as possible for the transformation to fully happen."

"Don't worry," he groaned. "I'll try to hold on as long as I possibly can. I'm enjoying this too much. Who knows when I'll have the opportunity again."

She laughed softly. "Soon. There are still my sisters."

He didn't remember her leaving him. When he awoke, the whole thing seemed unreal. Maybe he just dreamed about having sex with Seel. Looking around, he saw only two of the girls lying beside him.

He rose and walked to the door, looked outside, but the tunnel was empty. Then he realized that he was completely nude.

Hearing him move around must have awakened the girls. Both of them got up at the same time.

Sheera and Pteer.

"Where is Seel?" he asked.

They gave him a strange look. "Don't you remember?"

Sheera's question and his nudity made him feel uncomfortable. "Remember what?"

"Seel changed last night. You helped her, remember?"

"We..." He felt his cheeks heating up. "You know?" he asked, looking at Sheera. Somehow, he'd always felt closer to her than her sisters.

"Yes," she said. "We watched."

"What? You watched." He wiped his forehead, embarrassment making him suddenly perspire. "I'm sorry you saw that. She seduced me."

Sheera laughed gently and came up to him. "No need to apologize. It is good. I am happy you helped my sister. I hope you'll do the same for me and Pteer." She stood on tiptoes and kissed him.

He went over to the bed and sank onto it. "Wow," was all he could say. Looking up at Sheera who stood in front of him, smiling, he shook his head. "I don't know what is going on here. Am I imagining all of this?"

She knelt in front of him and touched his cheek. Her purple eyes studied him solemnly. "Do you feel attracted to me, Stonewall?"

He nodded, not trusting his throat to speak.

"How would you describe this attraction?"

"I think I love you." His voice sounded almost harsh.

"But I'm not even of your species," she said softly. "How can you love me?"

He shrugged. "I don't know. I just do."

She smiled. "This might sound strange, but I love you, also."

"Then how can you be so calm after you saw me screwing your sister," he cried out in agony.

"You couldn't help it. When we change, our bodies exude a mass of pheromones no male can resist. It wasn't your fault."

"But I enjoyed it, don't you understand?"

"I am glad you enjoyed it. That means Seel also enjoyed it, and you helped make her transition easy. It is not always pleasant for us." She sat down beside him. "Promise me, you will help Pteer the same way. With joy. Promise me that."

He mopped his forehead again. "If that is your wish. What about you?"

Laughing, she leaned against him. "I know we will both experience great pleasure. I will try my best to make it happen, for both of us."

"So where is she?" he asked.

"She left, trying to find help to get us out of here."

"I don't understand. How can she go for help? We're half a mile off the ground."

"She found a way, believe me." Sheer put her arms around his neck. "I am glad you are here, Stonewall."

He watched Pteer kneel in front of him and didn't pull back when she bent forward to plant a soft kiss on his lips. "There is no shame in what you did," she said softly. "I am looking forward to our joining. I am happy it will be a pleasant one for me."

"May I enter this happy home?"

Stonewall looked at the door and saw Wong standing in the opening. "Sure, come on in."

Wong stepped through and gave Stonewall a puzzled look. "Are you in the habit of sleeping nude, or am I interrupting something?"

Stonewall chuckled, getting used to feeling embarrassed. "Neither. I'm just airing out my clothes."

"It's none of my business," Wong said, watching Stonewall slip into his clothes. "Remember Maisoneuve telling you yesterday that he'd be going to the garden? Well, he did. About an hour ago. I think he's being controlled or something. Want to come with me to check up on him?"

"Sure." Stonewall rose to his feet. "I won't be long," he said to the girls, and then he followed Wong out of the room.

They found the room that held the garden and peeked inside.

"Son-of-a-bitch!" Wong cursed softly beside him.

Stonewall couldn't see anything unusual at first, just the pool and the colorful vegetation, but then he heard moaning sounds and saw something moving behind one of the yellow glowing shrubs.

Wong entered the garden and headed for the shrub.

Stonewall trailed slowly behind him.

They stayed in the shadow of a tall shrub, but they had a clear view of the scene in front of them.

Maisoneuve lay in the embrace of a voluptuous woman. His naked buttocks moved steadily between her spread thighs.

"The bastard wasn't lying," Wong whispered.

"We should leave," Stonewall whispered back. He didn't feel right watching another man having sex. To him, it was a personal, private matter between two people. It shouldn't be made into a spectacle.

"I want to see that woman's face," Wong said. "Stay a few moments longer. There is no harm."

They watched with fascination as Maisoneuve fucked the unknown woman. As far as Stonewall could see, she was human, but now he was also curious to see her face.

Maisoneuve shuddered suddenly and let out a triumphant shout. Then he left the woman's embrace and stood up. A little shakily at first, but then he stood there, smiling at the woman. "Now that's what I call a satisfying fuck." Maisoneuve laughed. "This one was even better than yesterday, wouldn't you say?"

The woman also got to her feet. She was fleshy, with wide hips and big breasts. When she turned, Stonewall noticed her fat buttocks. "It was," she said. "Will you be back tomorrow?"

"Sure will. Will you be alone, or are you going to bring your friend again?" He chuckled. "She made me feel good, too. You both did."

The woman laughed softly and turned to walk away. "Bring your friend tomorrow, and I'll bring two of mine," she said over her shoulder.

Stonewall watched her walking toward the exit. There was something about her that didn't look right. The closer she came to the exit, the more the outlines of her body seemed to waver, as if he were looking at her through a glass filled with water.

"Let's follow her," he said to Wong, after seeing Maisoneuve getting into the pool. The woman disappeared through the opening, and the two men hurried to catch up with her.

When they entered the tunnel on the other side, they didn't see the woman. Instead Stonewall stared at the back of a white, fat creature waddling away from them.

"That looks like a giant slug," Wong whispered beside him. "What happened to the woman?"

Things suddenly began to fall into place in Stonewall's mind. "That is the woman," he said, shuddering.

"What do you mean?"

"When you suggested that another species might be occupying the upper floors of this place, I started to think. I've heard of many species on Earth that have the ability to mimic other creatures. Either for protection or just simply to survive. Some are parasitic and feed off the species they mimic. I think that's what we have here."

"Giant slugs that look like Humans?"

"Or Ants, whatever the occasion demands. Another curious thing. I've seen two of those Slugs before. In the alien ship. They were dead, but they were definitely passengers. The Ants carried a number of large boxes out of the wreck. It seems to me that ship didn't come to this planet by accident. It just missed its landing site. Those Ants went to the crash site with a purpose."

"To pick up those boxes?" Wong wondered. "What about your new friends, the alien females? Maybe they were also meant to be delivered here?"

While they talked, the creature disappeared into another tunnel.

Wong suddenly burst out laughing. "Wait till I tell Maisoneuve that he fucked a slug. He'll get a kick out of that."

"I don't believe he'll be amused. He probably won't believe you. I wouldn't. Even now, after seeing it with my own eyes." Stonewall cursed loudly. "I wonder if this was the same creature I mistook for Lucinda? Damn it! I fucked one of them!" He stared at Wong who grinned. "It isn't funny. It's disgusting. That's what it is. I should have smelled something was wrong. She told me she came in a ship. Lucinda would never have come after me. We had already parted ways and not exactly on good terms. But damn it, she gave me a good fuck, as good as the real Lucinda."

"I wonder why they're doing it," Wong mused. "I mean, why are they seeking intercourse with someone not of their species?"

"Perhaps there are none of their males here," Stonewall suggested.

[9]

"Is anything wrong?" Sheera asked when she saw him studying her.

"I was just wondering if there is anything you may want to tell me?" Stonewall said.

"Like what?"

"Like..." He shrugged. "Did you know you would be coming to this planet? Maybe visit these giant bugs?"

"I don't understand."

The way she looked at him, Stonewall felt inclined to believe her. Even though her face didn't show much emotion, her eyes spoke for her. She really didn't know what he meant.

"Today I saw a creature similar to the two passengers on the ship that brought you here. Like a huge slug. It changed its shape, became a woman. Do you know anything about creatures like that?"

Sheera held her breath. "Yes, of course I do. They are called *Accilla*. They can change the shape of their bodies, mimicking other species. Sometimes they live undetected among others. Sometimes they show themselves in their original shape, like the two on the ship. They are not very numerous."

"How dangerous are they?"

"Not much is known about them because of their ability to

conceal themselves, but I don't believe they are hostile." Her purple eyes seemed larger than usual. "They are here?"

"I think so. We've seen at least one of them."

"And you believe we knew about that?" She shook her head. "Your assumption is wrong. As I told you, we were kidnapped. We didn't know anything about this planet being our destination. Why would the *Snaar* bring us here?"

Stonewall shrugged. "These *Snaar*, are they traders?"

She laughed. "That and many other things. Most of them not good."

"Well, there may be your answer. You were just something to trade. There is no reason to believe, though, that you were meant to be traded on this planet. Remember the long boxes the *Bugeyes* carried out of the ship? I think they were the merchandise to be delivered."

"What did those boxes contain?"

"I have no idea. Food maybe? Tools? Who knows?"

Someone walked by the room. Stonewall went to the door and looked out in time to see Maisoneuve heading for his room. He stepped into the tunnel and followed him. Maisoneuve either heard or sensed him, because he stopped and turned around.

"Hey, Stonewall. What's on your mind?"

Stonewall gave him a tiny smile. "Did you have a good time?" he asked the older man.

Puzzled, Maisoneuve asked, "A good time? What do you mean?"

"Wong and I checked on you this morning. We saw you in the park, having sex with a woman."

Maisoneuve grinned. "Oh that. Yeah, that was great. She's a woman I met once in a bar. I'll see her tomorrow. She promised to bring friends. You want to come?"

"Have you ever wondered how she came to be here on this planet? Here in this particular place?"

"I have given it some thought. I think these *Bugeyes* have the ability to make dreams a reality. How?" He shrugged. "I don't know, and it doesn't really matter. Maybe they move from one dimension to another, take events that might have happened in another dimension or universe and make them real. We know nothing about the universe, about reality and dreams. Maybe instead of developing technology, they developed the powers of their minds."

"Interesting theories, but I believe you are totally off track. There is no mystery here, no manipulating of minds and dimensions. The woman you fucked is not human. She belongs to a species known as *Accilla,* a race of mimics, possibly parasites."

Maisoneuve must have noticed the pity and even hint of smugness in Stonewall's voice and expression. "How the hell do you know this? You're just guessing, the same as me."

"No guess. I have proof. There were two of the creatures in the ship, dead, and also a number of large boxes, which the *Bugeyes* unloaded and brought here. Besides, Wong and I saw the woman change back to her original form after she left you. That's how we know."

Maisoneuve stared at Wong who had come out of their room. "Is that true?"

Wong nodded. "It's true. I've seen it with my own eyes."

Maisoneuve shook his fist. "Damn it all." Then he stared at Stonewall. "You fucked one of them. How did you enjoy it?"

"Best fuck I ever had," Stonewall admitted, reluctantly. "But in my defense, I didn't know it wasn't my ex-girlfriend. I acted in good faith. And, I must add, I was extremely horny."

"So was I. We were both victims." His face took on a dreamy look. "Although, I have no regrets. I'd probably do it again. As long as that creature looks like Elmira, I'll fuck her until I drop from exhaustion."

"If you see what she really looks like, you may change your mind," Wong said. He glanced at Stonewall. "You want to go exploring? Maybe we can find their hideout and confront them. Tell them we know their game and to let us go, before our people come and punish them."

Maisoneuve snorted, clearly in contempt. "Forget about being rescued by our people. They've written us off as being dead. They'll never be able to enter this fortress. The Ants will cut them to pieces before they're able to even come close." He seemed to make up his mind. "However, I'll come with you. I'm just as curious as you are."

Stonewall peered into the room he shared with the girls. Sheera and Pteer looked at him anxiously.

"We're going to see if we can locate our captors. Maybe we can negotiate our way out of here."

"Be careful," Sheera said softly.

"Don't worry. I will. If what you told me about these *Accilla* is true, they won't harm us. We want to find out what they want from us."

The tunnels were empty of movement.

"They must all be in the upper floors," Wong said.

One of the tunnels looked higher and wider than the rest, so they decided to take that one.

"We could easily get lost," Stonewall said. He pulled out his pocketknife and scratched an arrow into the wall to show which way back to their *apartment*, as Maisoneuve called it. He kept doing this at regular intervals. The tunnel ended in another large cavern.

It wasn't empty.

Stonewall almost whistled when he saw the furnishings. Tables and chairs fabricated from wood stood on one side. Obviously not made for human bodies, but there was no mistaking their purpose. Some chairs were occupied. The beings sitting in the chairs were dressed in clothing made from leather and cloth. At first look, their shape seemed humanoid, but at closer examination, the real form of the creatures became evident.

The bright light, shining through a huge opening in one wall, left no doubt.

They were giant slugs.

It was eerily silent in the room, but they appeared to be engaged in conversation, moving short limbs, which grew from their upper bodies, the way Humans do when talking to each other.

They stopped suddenly, all of them turned to look in the direction of the tunnel in which the three men lurked.

One of the slugs left its seat and came toward them, waddling on short, stubby legs.

"We know you are there," said a human voice. It sounded oddly familiar. "There is no need for you to hide."

Stonewall was the first to step into view. The other two followed him reluctantly.

The pudgy shapeless face of the creature began to quiver, mold itself, became human.

"You are not supposed to be up here," the creature said, visibly forming the words with a pair of full lips.

Stonewall stared at the face, fully formed now.

"Lucinda," he said involuntarily. The head and face looked grotesque on the shapeless body.

The creature smiled Lucinda's smile. "Hello, Terrex. Nice to see you again."

"Stop it!" Stonewall screamed and put his hands over his ears. "You are not Lucinda. Why are you doing this?"

"My apologies. I thought it would make you feel at ease."

"It horrifies me. Were you the one in the garden with me?"

Nodding, the creature said, "Yes. Did you get pleasure from our joining?"

"Does it matter? Did you?"

"I did. Pleasure and nourishment."

"Nourishment? What does that mean?"

"I took some of your blood. We need it to survive."

"Bloody vampires!" Maisoneuve cursed beside Stonewall. "I've heard of your kind."

"Yes, you have. We've been to the planet of you Humans." The creature smiled. "Humans are prolific breeders. Earth has always provided us with a good harvest."

"You call bloodsucking *harvesting*?" Stonewall shouted.

"It is only an expression. We never take anything without giving back. We take blood, but we give great pleasure. You and your companion can testify to that." The face of the creature seemed to flow and changed into that of a man.

"Is this better?" it said with a male voice.

All three men stared at the new face. It didn't inspire them much, either, to look into the half-formed face of their chief.

"Where do you get these images from?" Stonewall asked.

"From you. We can touch your mind and draw out information."

"You read our minds?" Wong sounded appalled. "I don't like anyone snooping around inside my mind. You should respect other being's privacy."

"We don't snoop. We just read your surface thoughts."

"The same thing."

"It is the way we communicate with each other. Come, sit with us and talk. We are anxious to hear news from the outside worlds."

They followed the creature to one of the tables. The other ones, who had been watching with apparent keen interest, turned away and went back to their own conversations and drinking from small plastic containers.

"It is our rest period," explained their guide, speaking with Chief Farmer's voice. "And time to take the nourishment we've been waiting for. Sit down. The seats should be comfortable enough even for you."

After the Humans were seated, one of the Accilla brought them a pitcher with water and three cups. It also brought them a platter filled with fruit.

Their host took the small container already on the table and began sucking through a tube.

"What is that you're drinking?" Wong asked.

The creature released the tube and smiled. "Blood."

Wong shook himself, and Maisoneuve murmured something under his breath.

"Why are we here?" Stonewall asked.

"The *Uur* brought you."

"Who are the *Uur*?"

The creature stayed silent for a moment, and then it said, "You refer to them as *Bugeyes.*"

"Of course they brought us. Because you told them to."

"We didn't tell them anything. Their mission was to recover the supply of blood we ordered from the Snaar. We hoped it hadn't been destroyed when the ship crashed. It was unfortunate for you that you were present when the hunters found the ship."

Stonewall threw Wong and Maisoneuve a quick look. "You're telling us that the ship was headed here?"

"You are correct. It is our only connection to the rest of the galaxy."

"You are not native to this planet?" Wong asked.

With a chuckle, the creature said, "No, we are not. We are prisoners here, just like you."

"What the hell are you saying? Who is keeping you prisoners?"

"Not prisoners. We are exiles, but we might as well be prisoners. We are not allowed to leave this planet."

"Are we your prisoners?" Stonewall asked.

"No."

"Then let us leave here."

The creature shook its head. "It is not our decision to make. You'd better get back to your rooms. It is not safe up here for you."

"Who would want to harm us?"

"I cannot answer your question. Please, go back now." It rose, indicating with a short arm the direction they should be taking. "Go! Hurry!"

Something in the creature's demeanor kept them from protesting. Shoving a fruit into his pocket, Wong rose. "One never knows," he said to Stonewall and shrugged.

The three men walked briskly back into the tunnel they had come out of. They found their way back easily, not really needing the arrows Stonewall scratched into the wall, since they hadn't taken any side-tunnels.

The girls waited anxiously for Stonewall's return.

"Did you find a way out?" Sheera asked.

He shook his head. "The only things we found were more questions than answers."

[10]

Slugs that turned into Lucinda plagued his dreams that night. They mocked and laughed, their naked voluptuous bodies gyrating in front of him. When he tried to grab them, the slugs slithered away on short fat legs.

He awoke with a tremendous hard-on.

"Are you awake?" a female voice whispered.

"I am now."

"Good. Our time has come."

He saw two slim shadows on either side of him.

Sheera and Pteer.

Kneeling.

A pair of hands began tugging on his pants. Another on his shirt. He knew what they wanted. It didn't take him long to get undressed.

One of the girls giggled when she touched his stiff cock. "I can see you're ready for us." She straddled him, and, without any preliminaries, she sheathed him with her hot cunt. He didn't know which of the girls fucked him, but he didn't care, just pushed up, deep into her.

A loud sigh escaped him, and then a pair of warm lips covered his, kissed him hard. Soft breasts touched his chest.

He inhaled their heady scent, knew their bodies were flooding his senses with pheromones. Even had he wanted to resist their demands, his own desires left him no choice.

The girl bouncing in his lap cried out as a climax gripped her body. She sat quivering until it subsided then she lifted up and let her sister take her place.

He let her squirm above him, watched her experience a series of orgasms, suppressed his own yearning to release the pressure building up inside him. She left him to give her sister another turn with him.

"I want to be on top," he moaned, realizing he needed to take control if he wanted to last much longer.

"All right."

The girl released him and lay on the bed, her legs apart. He moved between them, put his organ between her thick pussy-lips and rubbed it slowly back and forth, giving himself time to relax the urge to come.

She wiggled her bottom. "Come on," she crooned, "put it back in. Don't let me get cold."

He complied with her wish, slid easily into her hot sheath. He fucked her slowly, enjoying every deep thrust, relishing every moment as her inner muscles caressed his engorged organ.

She let out little mewling sounds, like a kitten in pain, but he knew she was not hurting. Churning beneath him, she made it hard for him to fight his own craving. He didn't want it to end, wanted to give her sister the same pleasure she experienced.

When her movements slowed, he knew she was ready to give up her place.

"My need has been fulfilled," she said suddenly. "Now, help my sister to complete her transition."

He pulled out of her, still hard.

Sheera slithered underneath him, spread her legs wide. His eyes had adjusted enough to the darkness inside the room, and he could see her happy smile. Her arms went around his neck. He grabbed his penis and guided it into her waiting pussy. She pushed up when she felt him and took him deep into her.

"I am happy you saved your seed for me," she said softly. "I will nourish it inside my womb."

He didn't know what she meant, and he didn't care. His own need overpowered any rational thought, and giving himself up to his animal desires, he plunged his cock into her clutching cunt, fucked her hard and steady.

She matched his furious passion and hammered her body against his, crying out softly and uttering words in her native tongue.

Then came the time when he could not control the terrible pressure, and, with a harsh cry, he relaxed, felt his penis jump inside her, felt the hot liquid gushing out of him with a release so strong, he kept on shouting until it finally ended.

His breath rattled in his throat when he collapsed into her arms, lay gasping on top of her soft, warm body, cradled by her thighs and arms. Her hands moved gently across his back, stroking him. He became aware of crooning sounds, realized they came from Sheera.

"I love you," he whispered. Then he kissed her.

She kissed him back. "I love you, too," she said with a gentle voice.

They separated, but he kept his arm across her chest, as they lay beside each other, afraid she might leave him.

However, when he woke, he found himself alone. Both girls were gone.

———

As the day passed, he waited for them to return or for any signs as what might have happened to them, but they never came back. He began to question his memory. Did they ever really exist?

Maisoneuve and Wong came to visit him in the afternoon.

"Where are the girls?" Maisoneuve asked.

Stonewall tried not to show his uneasiness. Shrugging, he said, "I don't know. They were not here when I woke up." He didn't know if he should tell the men anything.

We fucked all night, and now they're gone.

How could he explain what went on between him and the alien females. He didn't understand what they meant when they told him about their transition into adulthood. He worried about them. Why would they leave him without explaining where they went? Sheera told him she loved him, but what did she mean when she spoke those words?

She was alien. Maybe it was just another way of saying *I love to fuck you.* He had no reason to believe there could be anything else but the physical joining of their bodies, without any emotional attachment.

"Could it be they are part of the mental games the *Bugeyes* are playing with us?" Maisoneuve speculated.

"I doubt that. Besides, it's those Slugs who are messing with our bodies and our minds. I don't believe the girls have anything to do with them. They are survivors of that crashed ship, remember?" Stonewall rejected the man's accusation.

"That ship brought fresh blood for the Slugs. You have only the word of those girls that they were prisoners."

Stonewall mulled over those words but could not accept the possibility that he may be the victim of some kind of plot. Shaking his head, he said, "Something has happened to them. I need to find out what."

All three men turned when they heard the commotion at the door. One of the *Bugeyes* entered the room.

Our queen wants to see you. Come!

The words sounded clear inside Stonewall's head, almost as if they were spoken aloud.

A number of the giant Ants waited for them in the tunnel. They formed a ring around the three Humans as they escorted them down the tunnel.

Coming out in the cavern, they marched across it and entered another tunnel. This one led down to the lower sections of the giant hill. After traveling through a maze of tunnels, always descending, they finally emerged in a room, almost as large as the one in the upper regions. Colorful woven carpets covered the cold walls and the floor.

On a raised dais, in a recliner made from woven branches, sat the Queen.

The three men were led in front of the dais and told to kneel.

"I'm not kneeling in front of a giant bug," Maisoneuve protested.

He let out a gasp of pain when one of their guards slapped him across the shoulders and forced him to his knees.

The Queen studied them with her multifaceted eyes. Then suddenly she spoke.

Inside their heads.

So you are the intruders in our midst!

A statement, not a question.

"We are not intruders," Stonewall spoke up boldly. "Your warriors took us prisoners, but you know that already."

I don't know anything. Only recently, I found out about your presence.

"But Your Highness, we were brought in front of you when we arrived here," Stonewall said.

Not in front of me. That was the imposter, the false queen. She rose from her reclining position and stood staring down at them with glittering eyes. *The ones who are holding you captive are parasites living among us.*

"You are aware of your uninvited guests?" Maisoneuve rose to his feet. When one of the guards moved to push him back down, the queen held up a three-fingered hand, and the warrior backed away.

Yes, I am aware of them. They are clever, pretending to be part of our hive. We've been tolerating them, but it is time we rid ourselves of the vermin.

Even though she spoke without a physical voice, her words sounded harsh in Stonewall's mind.

She stepped down from the dais. Towering above Stonewall, she said, *You will help me.*

Surprised and taken aback by her words, he said, "How can we help you? They are many. We are just three. There is not much we can do."

Something akin to laughter rang inside his head. *You are wrong. You can help. You have weapons superior to theirs and ours.*

Stonewall stared at her mask of a face. The hard chitinous shell looked cold, as if chiseled from stone. Her mandibles clicked dangerously close in front of him. Knowing she could take off his head with one snap of those sharp shears made him shrink away involuntarily.

You have nothing to fear from us. Soothing emotions seemed to accompany her words.

"We are without weapons," he said, spreading his arms.

Your people in the round hive have them.

"What do you know about our people?" Stonewall asked.

More than you're probably aware of. We've been watching you ever since you invaded our world.

We are not here as invaders," Stonewall said. "We are using your world as a place from which we can observe our enemies among the stars."

Your affairs are of no concern to us. We tolerate you because you have not displayed hostility toward us, but we know that you are not a peaceful race, and we hope that you will never use your terrible weapons against us.

"It is not in our interest to war against your kind," Stonewall assured her. "There is nothing to be gained by it. In fact, you have nothing to fear that we might lay claim to your world some day. There is nothing here that we can't find on other, more hospitable, worlds."

That is good, but there are others who desire our world.

She regarded them silently, and then she continued. *We are not technologically advanced. We use tools, primitive in your eyes but sufficient for us. We rely on our strength to perform most tasks. We have no means of traveling among the stars.*

Stonewall received the impression of a smile.

Yes, we are not ignorant about the worlds outside. We know there are many, and we know about other races, different from ours. Instead of developing technology, we have developed the powers of our minds.

Stonewall thought there was something wrong with his eyes when the outlines of her body began to waver. Something pulled inside his mind. He heard Maisoneuve and Wong shouting in surprise, and then he stared at the figure standing in front of him.

Tall, with the athletic body of a warrior-woman, dressed in body armor made from leather, she stood proudly, sword in one hand.

"You're one of them!" he said, gasping.

She shook her head. "No, I'm not. What you see is not real. I do not have the ability to change the shape of my body. I am manipulating your mind. Come touch me."

He saw her lips move; he seemed to hear the words coming out of her mouth. Reaching out, he gingerly touched her shoulder. It felt warm, her muscle tone hard, but resilient.

"What do you feel?" she asked.

"A human body."

"Be assured, what you touch is not human. My body is

unchanged. It is your mind that fools you into believing what you touch is real." She stepped closer, looked at him with dark, human eyes. Her lips formed a smile.

When he inhaled, her scent was that of a woman.

"You see, the intruders in our midst, and my kind are much alike. They change the shape of their bodies physically. We change ours inside your mind. It does not matter how it is done. We deceive others to see what is not really there. What makes us different from them is the fact that they use their ability to exploit. We don't."

"And what is your purpose?" he asked.

She chuckled. "Survival."

"I don't understand. You need to pretend you're human in order to survive?"

"Not human. There are many ferocious beasts on our world. Many view us as food. By making them believe we are not what they desire, we assure our survival."

A slight pulling inside his head, and he looked again at her original form.

"What is it you want from us?" Maisoneuve asked.

I told you before. Remove the parasites from our hive.

"How?"

Kill them!

"Hold it," Maisoneuve protested. "We can't just murder a bunch of intelligent beings who did nothing to us?"

They are keeping you prisoner.

"But they haven't harmed us. Not physically."

They will. It is just a matter of time. They need your blood.

"How do you know?" Maisoneuve sounded skeptical.

Are you forgetting I can look into their minds?

"You could let us leave right now, and we would be safe," Wong suggested.

I could, but that would not solve our problem. In addition, you would not be safe. The imposter queen controls the soldiers and hunters. You would be captured.

"Are you telling us you're not in control of this hive?" Stonewall asked.

An angry thought impulse stabbed into his mind.

That is correct. I control only a small group of loyal subjects. I, the rightful queen, am the usurper! Now do you understand?

"If you and your people are helpless against them, how can we be successful?"

You will ask the people in your hive for help.

"How?"

The queen turned away. She seemed to give instructions to the silent watching guards. Two of them turned and left the room through an opening in the back. They came back moments later, escorting three human-looking beings. Their nude bodies left no doubt about their gender.

Three females. Slim and tall, with generous curves. Long hair framed beautiful, narrow faces.

At first, Stonewall thought they had capes thrown across their shoulders, but then he saw that they were wings.

Colorful, butterfly-like wings folded behind them.

Staring into their faces, they seemed familiar. He shook his head, not believing what he thought, but when he saw their eyes, he somehow knew.

When the females saw the Humans, they gasped and let out small cries. One of them came running toward Stonewall. Her eyes glittered with purple fire.

"Sheera?" he asked.

"Yes." She flung her arms around his neck. "I'm sorry, our escape attempt failed."

He was still staring at her. "You look different," was all he could say.

"That is because now I am in my adult stage. I have shed the shell that kept me a juvenile. My transformation is now complete."

"You look so beautiful," he stammered, glancing at her sisters. "All of you. The hump on your back is gone. You have hair and...and wings."

She smiled happily. "That ugly hump hid our hair and wings."

My Sky-warriors caught them, saving them from certain death. The clouds hide many ferocious hunters. The Queen paused. *My warriors will accompany one and ensure she arrives safely at your hive. She will bring your warriors with their weapons.*

[11]

BACK IN THEIR CELL, STONEWALL, SHEERA, AND PTEER SAT ON the soft mattress of fluffy grass that served as their bed. Seel, the first one trying to escape, had volunteered to go with the Queen's Sky-warriors to find the station of the humans.

Stonewall studied Sheera's lovely features as she stood in front of him, still finding it hard to believe that this was the same hump-backed, baldheaded homely female he had fallen in love with. Her coarse face had smoothed out, leaving soft skin without any blemishes.

With the hump gone from her back, she now stood straight and tall, her body slimmer and more graceful than before.

Her wings were the strangest of all. Small and almost unobtrusive when folded behind her back, they looked magnificent when fully opened, shimmering with iridescent colors.

"Why are you staring at me like that?" she asked.

"I still can't believe how beautiful you are," he said. "And your wings! They seem so fragile. Can you really fly with them?"

Her laughter sounded full of joy. "As high as the winds will carry me. They are not as fragile as they appear."

"Do you think Seel will be able to find the station of my people?"

"The Queen has assured me her warriors know where your *Hive* is located." She looked at him gravely. "But are your people willing to kill the *Accilla* in cold blood?"

He shook his head. "We are not murderers. A compromise will have to be found." His gaze rested on her naked body. Remembering their lovemaking, he felt a gentle fluttering in his loins.

She noticed his look and smiled. Squatting down and reaching out with one slim hand, she said, "Do you still find me attractive?"

"More so than before," he told her.

"The pheromones my body exudes are not as strong anymore," she said, visibly pleased with his answer.

"Do women of your species always walk around in the nude? I mean, the wings must be a problem when it comes to wearing clothes."

"Women of our species wear clothing like any other civilized race. The wings are no problem." She smiled and gave him an inquiring look. "The reason we are naked is because we have no proper clothing. Does it offend you to see me this way?"

He broke into loud laughter. "Offend me? Are you kidding? No real man is ever offended by the sight of a lovely naked woman. Disturbed? Yes, but never offended."

"Why disturbed?"

He felt the blood staining his face and became aware of a sudden pulsing in his penis. "Despite our grave situation, I feel like grabbing you, kissing your lush lips and then making passionate love to you. For hours and hours."

"How about me?" Pteer asked, giving him an impish smile.

His eyes traveled over her nude form, finding her as desirable as Sheera. "What do you think?" he asked.

Both females laughed merrily. "The night is long. We have nothing to do but wait."

They watched him as he undressed. Naked, he sat on the bed, looking expectantly up at them. Sheera moved closer, stood wide-legged in front of him, her pink slit almost touching his nose.

Putting his tongue into her slit, he began licking her gently. She let out a little moan and took hold of his head, pressing her hairless mons pubis into his face. She tasted sweet, not salty like Lucinda, and he lapped up her discharge. He cupped her buttocks, enjoying their firm roundness in his hands.

She pushed gently on his head, while lowering herself to the ground. He stretched out on his back. Sheera squatted on his face and moved her lower body slowly back and forth. His lips were almost glued to her sweet cunt, his tongue pushed deep into her.

Somebody straddled him. Knowing it was Pteer, his hard cock throbbed with anticipation. Her pussy-lips grabbed the tip of his straining member, began teasing it with slow motions of her soft, slippery clit.

He moaned loudly, his fingers digging into Sheera's moving buttocks, when he felt his penis sliding into Pteer's liquid sheath.

Pteer rode him with gusto while he tongue-fucked Sheera.

Both women lifted off simultaneously. Sheera knelt on the floor, presenting her buttocks. Her wings unfolded and rested on either side of her, like a colorful silk cloak. Pteer joined her sister on the floor, her pert buttocks up.

He stared at the two pairs of pink pussy-lips beckoning to him from underneath creamy round globes. Driven by pure lust, he knelt behind Sheera and put his hand between her slightly spread thighs, stroking her pussy with a gentle finger. Then he put his penis into the crease between her soft buttocks, rubbing it back and forth.

She pushed her bottom higher. His rigid penis slipped into the space created by her spread thighs and, pushing forward, he slid into her greased sheath. Snapping her hips furiously, she held his pole in a tight grip, moved over it with incredible speed. A loud cry announced her approaching orgasm. She stopped moving, shook in his hands as the waves of pleasure washed through her.

He pulled out of her and moved over to Pteer, shoved his cock into her with one mighty thrust. Unlike her sister, she held still, let him take control. He began moving in and out of her warm sheath, slowly increasing his tempo until his hips hammered into her soft buttocks with furious strokes.

He wanted to save himself for Sheera but lost the battle. His climax rolled over him like a hurricane, and with a triumphant shout, he exploded inside Pteer's quaking tight cunt.

Sheera bent over him and kissed him gently.

"Sorry," he apologized. "I couldn't hold it any longer."

She laughed and kissed him again. "Pteer is my sister. I am happy if she gave you pleasure."

He flopped onto his back and sighed. He loved Sheera, but he didn't feel guilty about having fucked her sister, especially since they didn't seem to mind.

The women rose, and Stonewall watched, fascinated as they folded their wings into a tight bundle, not unlike a backpack. He could easily see that, by wearing loose clothing and padding in the right places, they would have no problem hiding their wings should they find it necessary.

"Can you lie on your back?" he wondered loudly.

"Yes. Why do you ask?"

He grinned, giving Sheera a leering look. "Maybe later we can do this again, but this time I'd like to be cradled by your soft thighs and feel your breasts against my chest."

"Why not now?" Pteer asked.

He pointed to his limp member. "He needs to recover first. You wore him out."

THE NEXT MORNING, WHEN HE LOOKED FOR MAISONEUVE AND Wong, he didn't find them in their room. He had an inkling where they might be, and his assumption proved correct.

Entering the garden, he heard them before he saw them.

Both men were engaged in what could only be described as *uncontrolled fucking*.

Locked in the embrace of two females, it was plain to see that the men were under the influence of either a drug or mental stimulation. The alien females hadn't even bothered to form their bodies fully into human likeness.

Stonewall was appalled to see Maisoneuve plunging his penis into the organ of a creature half Slug and half Human. Her lower half was that of a woman, with thighs, nice buttocks, and a human-looking vagina. Even her breasts were full, firm, but her hands displayed only three fingers, and her feet ended in large suction-cups.

The face looked human, but not the rest of her head.

Maisoneuve didn't seem to mind. With his eyes closed, he moved rhythmically on top of the grotesque-looking alien female.

When Stonewall looked for Wong, he discovered him in the pool, pounding into the sex-organ of a giant Slug. Only her large buttocks seemed fully formed.

Wong's fingers dug into her round shapeless hips, making indentations in the soft white flesh.

Stonewall turned away, disgusted by the sight. He couldn't wait for the rescuers to arrive.

They came shortly after noon.

Sheera and Pteer lifted their heads at the same time.

"They are here," Sheera said, rising from the bed.

Stonewall followed the sisters as they rushed down the tunnel toward the room with the opening to the outside. They had barely entered the large room, when a shadow darkened the sky and then the familiar figure of Seer stepped into the room. Folding her wings, she came running to meet her sisters.

"Did you find my people?" Stonewall asked her.

She nodded.

"Where are they?"

She pointed to the opening. "Go, have a look."

When he carefully peered outside, he stared at the sight below with unbelieving eyes. A huge cylinder rested on the hard ground beside the Hive. Figures spilled from it. They rose into the sky on large, black wings, like a swarm of locusts.

"Who are they?" he asked, bewildered.

"They are our people," Seer said, giving him a pleased smile.

The first of them reached the opening and climbed through, folding black wings behind a powerful body dressed in dark leather. Definitely a male, judging by the wide shoulders and muscular arms. He wore a skullcap and high boots. A shiny sword-like weapon shimmered bright in his brawny hand.

He ignored the females and addressed Stonewall. "Are you the Human Terrex Stonewall?"

When Stonewall nodded, he looked at Sheera. "Your father sends his regards.

Sheera gave him a polite nod. Then she smiled. "I am happy to see you also, my brother."

She turned to Stonewall and said, "This is my brother Ajah. He is a great warrior."

More of the alien males crowded into the room. Each one carried a shiny sword.

"Seer told us about the bargain you struck with the Queen of the Uur," Ajah said. He turned, as if searching for someone. Then Stonewall saw another creature sailing into the room.

A giant Ant with wings. One of the Queen's Sky-warriors, Stonewall had no doubt.

Ajah walked up to the newcomer and seemed to converse with him. Coming back, he said, "I am going to meet with the Queen. I must know more about this bargain." Then he turned and followed the Sky-warrior.

Another of the winged males came to speak to Sheera and her sisters. "You will leave this place now," he told them, speaking the common Earth-language, obviously for Stonewall's benefit.

"Not without Stonewall," Sheera said.

He nodded. "We came here to rescue him and the other two Humans. Where are they?"

"They are probably still occupied with the *Accilla* females," Stonewall said. "I'll take you to them."

Maisoneuve and Wong were still copulating with the giant Slugs. Neither the two men nor the alien females were aware of the intruders until they were almost upon them.

The *Accilla* let out a hissing scream when they saw the winged warriors and pushed their human partners from them. They struggled to get away, but the warriors pointed their swords at them. A bright light left the gleaming weapons, enveloped the gross bodies of the Slugs.

Both fell into lifeless heaps onto the mossy floor.

"They're not dead." One of the warriors answered Stonewall's unspoken question. "We don't kill wantonly."

Maisoneuve and Wong followed Stonewall in a daze, obviously not really aware of their rescue. A few of the winged men were waiting for the three Humans to come back. As soon as Stonewall walked into the room, one of them waved him over. They strapped him into some kind of harness, which two of them attached to belts around their waists, and then they launched themselves out of the opening, dragging him with them. At first, he felt apprehensive, being carried by two creatures he didn't even know. They could just drop him if they felt like it, but his fears proved unfounded. They floated down on their giant wings and deposited him almost gently beside the huge cylindrical ship. When Stonewall unhooked the harness, he heard a familiar voice calling his name. He looked up to see Peters running toward him.

"Am I glad to see you unharmed, Stonewall!" Peters shouted excitedly. "We assumed you were dead, like Wong and Maisoneuve."

"I'm very much alive." Stonewall grinned when Peters clapped him on the shoulders. "So are Maisoneuve and Wong. They should be coming down soon. Maybe they're already on the ground somewhere."

"Tell me everything that happened." Peters seemed unable to contain himself.

"All in good time, my friend." Stonewall smiled, suddenly feeling very tired as the adrenalin rush abated. "There is someone I need to talk to."

He saw her slim form outlined against the sky as she spiraled down on shimmering butterfly-wings. She landed beside him on light feet.

"Stonewall," she said, a little out of breath. "Don't try to run away from me."

Peters stared at her nude body. "Who is this?" he asked, his voice catching in his throat.

"This is Sheera," Stonewall said. "You must have met her sister Seel. She's the one who came to the station."

"I never talked to her. Only the chief and the guy I brought back in the scooter did. He made it, by the way. He called his people, using our communication system. When the girl came, her people were already there. Apparently, they had been chasing the ship that crashed." He bent close to Stonewall. "Who is she anyway?"

"Remember those three females in the caskets?"

Peters nodded. "I remember them, but they were different. Homely. Almost ugly."

Stonewall laughed. "Sheera is one of those ugly females. I'll explain later."

He turned to Sheera and looked at her, suddenly lost for words. She noticed his discomfort and came into his arms.

"What now?" he asked with a low, shaking voice.

"Nothing changes," she said. "I love you."

"I love you too, but how is this going to end? You'll be leaving with your people, and I'll be going back to my job."

She stroked his cheek with gentle fingers. "I will ask my father to allow you to come to my planet. That is the only way it will work." She kissed him and looked into his eyes. "But only if you want to do that. I hope you will."

"My people will object," he said.

"Don't worry about that. My father is a powerful man on our world. A lord. He will request that your people send you as an ambassador to our planet." She laughed. "They will not refuse him."

"An ambassador? I think I'd like that." He laughed and hugged her. "Tell me, what is going to happen to the *Accilla*? Are you going to kill them all?"

She shook her head, suddenly serious. "No. They will be transported to their own planet. They have no right to be here."

"I am glad. I would not want to see them murdered. It would be wrong."

"Yes, it would be." She smiled. "They are not evil. All they want to do is survive, like all of us." She hooked her arm into his and dragged him toward the ship. "Come, I want you to meet my father. And don't let him intimidate you. Once you get to know him, you'll see he is not so bad."

The End

———

Keep reading to enjoy a preview of the first novel in
The Stonewall Chronicles
A NEW DAWN

"A NEW DAWN"
THE STONEWALL CHRONICLES, BOOK 1

When Master Scout Terrex Stonewall returns to Epsilon he finds much has changed in fifteen years. Humans are beginning to colonize the world of the Dinosaurs, but an alien species known as The Spiders challenges the Humans for possession of the planet. Stonewall must find out why before it is too late.

Note: *The story takes place 15 years after the events in 'Outpost Epsilon.'*

[1]

Terrex Stonewall experienced a feeling of déjà vu as he stepped out of the shuttle. Almost everything looked the same. In many ways not much had changed. The mushrooms were still as huge and intimidating and the air as humid and hot. Standing still for a moment, he took a few shallow breaths, letting his system get used to the stifling heat.

Outpost Epsilon had been his first assignment as a Scout for the Solar Union. As he stood looking around, he could hardly believe that fifteen years had passed since then.

He swallowed hard as suppressed memories rushed into his conscious mind. It was here on Epsilon where he fell in love with a Tangari girl.

Sheera. He never really forgot her.

Shrugging, he studied his surroundings. The original dome, which protected the outpost, was still there, but he saw three more domes, one of them larger than the others. All four domes were connected by tunnels.

The area around the domes had been cleared of vegetation and a large number of the giant mushrooms, allowing a good view of the sky overhead. Even the landing pads for the shuttles had been enlarged and paved.

A Builder-ship was parked near the largest dome. Construction robots were busy cleaning up the site. As far as Stonewall knew, the habitat was finished. The ship might move on to another part of Epsilon and begin building another settlement or it might possibly travel to a different planet. He didn't know its schedule and didn't really care.

This time, nobody came to greet him. He wondered how many members of the original crew were still around.

They had changed the entrance to the dome. Instead of a door, he saw a small building, like a guardhouse. His assumption proved correct. When he approached the dome, a door opened and a man wearing the brown uniform of the Scouts appeared. He carried a flash rifle, but he didn't act hostile.

Stonewall wore the same uniform, except his was adorned with a small bar on his left sleeve, proclaiming his rank as Master Scout.

"Welcome, sir," the guard said, saluting stiffly. "You've been expected."

Stonewall returned the salute and smiled. "I hope there's a cold beer waiting for me."

The guard gave him a strange look, his posture still rigid. "I'm not sure what you mean, sir."

Suppressing a chuckle, Stonewall said, "I have a feeling things have changed a lot. Relax. I'm not going to shoot you for not rolling out the red carpet as soon as I stepped off the shuttle."

"I still don't understand, sir."

Stonewall sighed. "Forget it, son. Just let me get out of this friggen greenhouse. I'm dying here."

"Sorry, sir." The guard didn't move. "I need to see your papers, sir."

"My papers?" It was Stonewall's turn to stare. "Didn't they brief you about me?"

"They did, but I still need to see your identification papers, sir."

Stonewall glared at him, irritated. "I am Master Scout Terrex Stonewall. I didn't come here for a vacation because I love it here so much. We used to call this place *Shithole* and I was happy when I finally left it after spending two friggen years evading oversized lizards and other hungry beasties. So be a good boy and step aside!"

Stonewall noticed the tightening of the young man's jaw muscles and the flickering in the brown eyes. He had to give him credit, because the man didn't flinch otherwise.

"I am aware of your name, sir, but it is my job to insure that you are really Master Scout Stonewall. I can do that only after looking at your papers and taking a retina scan."

Sighing again, Stonewall reached into his breast pocket. "You are a stubborn young man, but I guess you're only doing your job. I hope this is not an indication of the way things are run here now. I don't need any more aggravation." He pulled out his ID card and handed it to the guard.

The guard ran his wrist scanner over it and gave it back to Stonewall. Holding the scanner in front of Stonewall's face, he said, "Please, look into the screen." Satisfied, he nodded. "Go ahead, sir. Sorry for the inconvenience, sir." He saluted again and stepped aside.

Stonewall tipped his helmet and shook his head. "Welcome back to Epsilon," he murmured. Then he walked into the guardhouse and through the door on the other end.

He stepped into cool air and breathed deeply.

At least that hadn't changed.

When he looked up, he saw the sky above him as clearly as if the dome didn't exist, even though it looked solid from the outside. *Just a matter of bending the light.* He still remembered William Peters explaining it to him the first time he entered the protection of the dome. Since then he had been in similar habitats on other planets, but it didn't diminish his admiration for the brilliant minds that had invented and designed these marvels of engineering.

Walking toward the Administration building, he wasn't sure how he would be greeted. He surely hoped that the incident with the guard was not an indication of what he could expect. The new chief of the outpost may not be as lax as Chief Farmer had been. He could still hear the Chief's words the first time they met.

Call me Chief. We are not that formal around here.

Entering the building, he walked down the familiar corridor toward the office at the end. The man behind the desk looked up when Stonewall walked through the door.

First impressions are usually the most important. Stonewall didn't get much of an impression from the man. Of average height and weight, in his early forties, his dark hair cut in the usual fashion of the Scouts, he didn't look imposing. Neither did he emanate any power or anything that set him apart from the regular Scouts.

"You must be Chief Wallace," Stonewall said, holding out a hand.

Wallace ignored the outstretched hand. He looked at Stonewall with expressionless eyes. "And you must be Master Scout Terrex Stonewall," he said, his voice as expressionless as his face and eyes. "I was informed of your arrival."

Stonewall smiled thinly. Taking back his outstretched hand, he said, "I expected a warmer welcome, Chief Wallace. After all, I came here to investigate alleged violations of treaty agreements with the indigenous population. Why the hostility?" He was surprised at Wallace's apparent resentment. Even though they had briefed him about the new chief, he suspected they hadn't told him everything.

To Stonewall's surprise, Wallace actually allowed himself a small chuckle, but it didn't sound friendly. "How would you feel if they'd send someone to undermine your authority, Stonewall?"

"So that's what you assume the purpose for my visit is. Let me assure you…I'm not here to undermine your authority, Chief Wallace. And if for some reason you are afraid I might be looking for your job, relax. I have no such intentions. The two years I spent in *Hell*, one of the nicer labels we gave this planet, will last me a lifetime. I'm here only because I am an experienced tracker, I know this planet and I had a good relationship with the Uur queen." He put his duffle bag onto the floor and began rummaging in it. Pulling out a bottle, he handed it to Wallace. "I brought you a present. This is from Earth. Authentic too. It is over forty years old. I was told you appreciate good Scotch."

Wallace glanced at the bottle and then at Stonewall. His face and posture seemed to relax somewhat. "It's been a while since I had a glass of good Scotch. Alcohol is not allowed on the outposts. You are aware of that, aren't you? How did you manage to smuggle a bottle through controls?"

Stonewall grinned. "Did you forget that I am a Master Scout? I'm not only good at finding things. I'm also good at hiding them. Take a look at the label."

"Dinosaur repellant," Wallace read. He shook his head and

chuckled. "Maybe you're not such a bad sort after all, Stonewall. Will you share a drink with me?"

Stonewall sank into the only chair in the room and sighed. "I thought you'd never ask. I don't mind a good stiff drink once in a while myself." He removed his helmet and wiped his forehead. "There was a time when I didn't drink alcohol, but time changes a man."

"Yes, it does," Wallace agreed.

Looking around the office, Stonewall said, "This office hasn't changed much since I was here last. You haven't even removed Chief Farmer's pictures."

Wallace sighed heavily. "I haven't had a chance to do much of anything since I took over Farmer's position. Too bad about him. He was a good man."

"He did have his good qualities." Stonewall watched Wallace take two glasses and a corkscrew from a drawer. It seemed that alcohol did make its way into the outpost at times.

Wallace took his time removing the cork from the bottle. He sniffed it and smiled. "Reminds me of the time I spent with my grandfather in Scotland. He taught me how to drink this stuff." Carefully, he poured two glasses and handed one to Stonewall. "Slainte Mhath."

"Slainte Mhor," Stonewall said solemnly. He downed his glass, tried not to flinch when the potent liquid ran down his throat.

Wallace closed his eyes for a moment. When he opened them, he regarded Stonewall silently. "Thank you, Master Scout. Maybe I misjudged you."

"It wouldn't be the first time someone read me wrong." Stonewall smiled, leaning back into his chair. "I'm curious, Chief Wallace. What exactly happened to Chief Farmer?"

Wallace shrugged. "I think he just got tired of this place." He squeezed the cork back into the bottle and got up to put the bottle into a small cabinet in the corner. Then he picked up a blue-shimmering many-faceted sphere from his desk. "You know what this is, don't you?"

Stonewall nodded. "A sapphire. You could buy yourself a small space ship with that one."

"Anywhere else but on Epsilon. This precious stone and others are found in abundance on this planet. The Uur mine them and shape them. They are masters when it comes to cutting gems. Of course, there are plenty of prospectors now on Epsilon who spend most of their time in the jungle digging for precious stones. The Union controls the export of these gems. Anyone smuggling them off planet is severely punished." Wallace stared at Stonewall. "There are some people out there who dispute the Union's right to control the gems and the drugs. Some very powerful people. It's all politics, you know. Farmer tried to interfere in the politics and he was caught in the crossfire. Pirates and drug dealers are another problem. We haven't been able to prevent every ship from landing in the remote regions and trying to make deals with the Uur. Some of those deals end up badly…for the Uur."

"Where is Farmer now?"

"I don't know. Maybe he's rotting on some prison planet. They took him away in chains." Wallace lowered his voice. "His reward for being a faithful servant of the Union for twenty years. I wonder what they have planned for me."

"You are certain it was a Union ship that took Farmer away?" Stonewall asked.

"It had no markings, except for its black color. The soldiers who picked him up wore the black uniforms of the Solar Union Special Forces."

"Nobody asked any questions?"

"You don't argue with members of the SUSF." Wallace chuckled grimly.

"Where were you when it happened?" Stonewall asked.

"In the office next to this one. I was Chief Farmer's assistant, in my second month of my one-year contract. That was two years ago. They told me if I wanted to rise in the hierarchy of the Scouts I would accept the position of Chief of the outpost. By the way, I'm also the Governor of Epsilon."

"Governor? Hmm."

"Don't let the title fool you. I have very little powers. I'm just a representative of Earth."

"Well, it's a title, but I detect some reluctance on your part," Stonewall said.

"I have a problem with being forced into doing something that may never have been my ambition. Besides, anywhere else would have been acceptable but not on this forsaken hellhole."

"You could have declined."

Wallace shrugged. "I could have but then what? I'm forty-two. Too old to start another career. They would have stashed me away on some other frontier world, worse than this one."

Stonewall shuddered a little, remembering the four months he spent on Snowball, a world of ragged mountains, ice storms, and continuous volcanic eruptions. "I know what you're talking about," he said. "As hard as it is to imagine, but there are actually worse places out there than Epsilon."

"You are right, it is hard to imagine." Wallace smiled.

Stonewall rubbed his chin. "If you are so unhappy with your job why would my arrival worry you? I might want to undermine your authority? I don't quite understand that."

"Actually, it is not my authority I'm worried about. I resent the fact that they presume I am not capable of handling the situation with the natives."

"I don't believe that is the case, Chief Wallace." Stonewall leaned forward, dropped his voice to a confidential level, as if afraid someone might hear his next words. "We have a problem. The Spiders have a battleship at the edge of this system."

Wallace's eyes widened. "This is the first time I hear of it. Why haven't we detected it?"

"The ship's been there for a month. It is just beyond reach of Epsilon's detection net."

"What do they want?"

"Epsilon."

"Epsilon?" Wallace almost shouted it, his voice echoed from the walls of his office. When he saw Stonewall's brows lift, he continued almost in a whisper, "Are they insane? Why would they send a battleship to a system that has nothing they ever wanted?"

Stonewall smiled at the other man's short outburst. "It is true Epsilon had nothing to offer them…until now."

"Like what?"

"Ancient ruins."

"Those ruins are evidence that a reptilian race once inhabited this planet." Wallace searched Stonewall's face. "Is there something you are not telling me?"

"Apparently, one of the mining companies unearthed ruins older than the ones of the reptilian races. Much older. Epsilon may be one of the birthplaces of the Spider race."

"I thought the Spiders originated in the Arcturus System?"

"Possibly not. The race of the Spiders is far older than humanity. Arcturus is probably just one of the systems they colonized long before Humans climbed out of the trees and began walking erect." Stonewall laughed. "We are newcomers to the denizens of Space. Even the dinosaurs are older than Humans. Much older."

Wallace shook his head. "Assuming Epsilon is a planet the Spiders originated from, what would they want with ancient ruins? Are they saying we are desecrating the bones of their ancestors? Even if there were any, they became dust a long time ago." He chuckled. "We've had that problem with many indigenous people on Earth. Maybe we should watch out for angry Spider spirits?"

Stonewall didn't find any humor in Wallace's remark, remembering the disappearance of the holy burial grounds of his own Iroquois ancestors. "We don't know anything about the Spider's spiritual beliefs," he said. "They gave no reason. My real mission here is to find out why they are risking an interstellar war with the Humans over a planet that is not hospitable to their kind."

"What is the Union doing about it in the meantime?"

"A Union Battle Cruiser is on its way to Epsilon. They're also sending two hundred Union Troopers."

"I'm afraid to ask where they'll be stationed." Wallace stared. "But I'm asking anyway."

Stonewall chuckled. "I understand you have a brand new bubble just waiting to be filled."

"Not with soldiers. It was supposed to be training facilities for rookie Scouts." Wallace rose and walked over to his cabinet in the corner. Taking out the bottle of Scotch, he said, "I need another drink. How about you?"

Stonewall nodded. "Maybe a small one."

———

Stonewall received a startling surprise after Chief Wallace said, "I'll have someone take you to your quarters."

The man who walked in was older than the last time he'd seen him, fifteen years to be exact, and his presence did come unexpectedly, but Stonewall would have recognized his lanky form anywhere.

"Peters?" He peered into the man's face. "What the hell are you doing here?"

Peters grinned. "I could ask you the same question. I thought you married that Tangari girl and by now you'd have at least half a dozen children."

A cloud settled over Stonewall's features momentarily. "Things didn't happen the way I hoped. Her father did not approve of his daughter's marriage to a Human." He smirked. "In the eyes of the Tangari Humans are physically handicapped because we don't have wings."

"At least our children are beautiful and not homely like theirs." Peters shook himself. "I still remember the ugly humps on the backs of those girls." He smiled. "Of course, that didn't seem to bother you."

"You have to admit those girls were beautiful after their metamorphosis." Stonewall chuckled ruefully. "I really did love Sheera."

"I guess your ambition of becoming an ambassador didn't work out either?"

"It was never my ambition. The whole idea came from Sheera. It would have given me a chance to be near her and things could have developed from there." Stonewall smiled. "That is all in the past. It wasn't meant to be." He scrutinized the other man. "Enough of me. How about you? Why are you here and not with your wife and children? As I remember, you left the Scouts two months after I arrived here."

"Yes, I did." Peters nodded. "We left Earth to settle on *Kolibri*…to start a new life. A year later our settlement was hit by raiders. They murdered nearly half the population. My wife and son were among those killed." A twitch ran through his face. "I couldn't protect my own family. I was on the other side of the planet surveying land designated for a new colony."

"I'm sorry about your wife and son. Did they ever get those responsible?"

Peters worked his jaws in a visible effort to control his emotions. "I joined the Enforcement Patrol for a couple of years to give me an excuse to rid the universe of vermin like that. A few of us survivors from *Kolibri* formed a special unit and we searched for the raiders."

"Did you find them?"

"We did. We destroyed the whole fucking asteroid they used as their base and killed every last one of them, including their families," Peters said grimly. "I'm not proud of what we did, but their sons and daughters would have grown up to become pirates like their parents. It was justified." He gave Stonewall a sad smile. "Unfortunately, it didn't make much of a difference, did it? There are still plenty of criminals roaming the space ways."

Stonewall shrugged. "At least you got your revenge. That is something."

"Yes, it is." Peters looked at Wallace. "Sorry, Chief, to bore you again with my past. It's just…"

Wallace waved his hand in dismissal. "I understand. Seems you and Master Scout Stonewall are old acquaintances. I wasn't aware of that."

"We knew each other only for two months," Stonewall said, glancing at Peters. "But we became good friends during that short time."

"Good to hear that." Wallace heaved a sigh. "It means you two will get along. Peters happens to be the liaison officer between the Uur nation and the Humans. He can be your guide if you so wish."

"I have no objections." Stonewall smiled at Peters. "A friendly face will make my job much easier."

"I'm looking forward to working with you again. At least this time you're not the greenhorn you were back then." Peters turned to walk out of the door. "Come on, I'll show you to your executive suite." He laughed. "I believe I used the exact same words the last time, but don't worry, it won't be the dormitory. We have made some progress since then and as I understand a room has been prepared for you."

"Anything will be better than my last assignment," Stonewall said as he walked beside Peters. "Three months of traveling on the hard back of a giant worm and sleeping in a tent at night listening to howling, screeching, and the flapping of winged horrors reminded me how comfortable and safe it is in a domed habitat like this one."

Peters chuckled. "In that case it will be a picnic when you travel again on the surface of Epsilon."

"As long as it is inside a rover," Stonewall said, smiling. He knew Peters was kidding. Traveling on Epsilon was anything but a picnic. The two years he spent here had seemed like a lifetime. When he finally left, he vowed never to return. But thirteen years away from this place had softened the memories. Besides, his superiors did not give him a choice when they handed him the assignment.

Peters took him through the connecting tunnel to the next bubble. They stepped onto a street paved with molten and fused rocks. Two-story buildings lined the street on either side. The umbrellas of nearby mushrooms loomed over the buildings and the invisible shell gave the illusion of a small town nestled in a fairy tale setting.

Stonewall stopped for a moment to take in the peaceful scene. "Like a picture out of a children's storybook," he said.

"I never looked at it that way," Peters said. "This is where the enlisted men live with their families. The unmarried men still live in a common room in the first bubble. Not all of the apartments are occupied. One of them has been reserved for you."

When Stonewall looked to the end of the street, he saw the entrance to another tunnel. Beyond that, the opaque rounded surface of the third habitat rose out of the ground.

"That is our latest addition," Peters explained when he noticed Stonewall's object of interest. "You've probably seen the Builder-ship outside. They sure didn't take much time with this one. A human construction crew wouldn't be able to build something like this in such a short time. And without mishaps. So far, this last shell is unoccupied."

"Not for long," Stonewall said. "Expect two hundred Union soldiers. They should be arriving within days."

"Why would the Union send soldiers to Epsilon? Are we at war with someone?"

"Not yet." Stonewall's expression was grim. "The Spiders have expressed a sudden interest in Epsilon."

"The reason?"

"Ruins. Let me fill you in over dinner. I am thirsty and hungry. Is Tommy, the cook, still around?"

"No. He took his lover Garth and left Epsilon about four years ago. We haven't heard from either of them since. The new chef is a woman. She is quite capable, and so is her kitchen staff. All females." He winked. "I understand they do more than cook meals for the men. Anyway, those are only rumors."

"Rumors again? Like the ones about Tommy and Garth?" Stonewall laughed.

"The ones about Tommy and Garth were true," Peters protested.

"What about the kitchen staff? You're not sure about them?"

Peters shrugged. "Never felt the need for their services. After my wife died, I lost all interest in women. My career is all I'm thinking of." He glanced at Stonewall. "And you?"

"I have needs and I have no problem with searching out female companionship. I never say no to a willing woman." Stonewall smiled. "There is only one condition. She has to be beautiful."

"Of course," Peters said dryly. "Beautiful women are better lovers than ugly ones, I suppose."

"I'm not saying that. The way I look at it, making love is like eating. A good-looking plate of food enhances the appetite. Does the food taste better?" Stonewall shrugged. "Maybe."

"How about closing your eyes when you eat?"

Stonewall punched Peters on the arm and laughed. "And rob myself of one of my senses? Never!"

"You are a demanding man, my friend. I hope your expectations are always met."

Stonewall grinned. "Not always. Maybe that is the reason I haven't had much luck lately."

"I'm afraid your luck won't change greatly here." Peters stopped in front of one of the buildings. "Here we are. Your quarters are on the first floor."

They entered the building through the main entrance. Each building contained four apartments. Peters pointed to the door on the left. "That one is yours." He opened it and made a motion for Stonewall to go through the door. "There are no locks." He smiled. "No privacy, either."

Stonewall looked around in the apartment. It was surprisingly spacious, considering space was at prime inside the bubbles. "It seems a shame that one man should occupy this much room," he commented.

"It wasn't meant for only one man. We just happen to have a few still empty. All of these buildings are fairly new. Not all the families have arrived yet. In a few months from now these will all be occupied."

Stonewall shook his head. "Much has surely changed since I left. I still remember the cramped quarters we lived in, sharing one room with a dozen other guys. I suppose some of the families have children?"

"They do."

Stonewall didn't really have to ask the next question. He could guess, but he was curious anyway. "What about their education?"

"Oh, that is taken care of. We have a classroom and a teacher. There are only nine children here, but we are expecting six more. She'll have her hands full."

"She?"

"Yes. The teacher is a woman. Miss Leroux. Simona Leroux."

Stonewall threw his duffle bag onto the small couch. Looking at his watch, he shrugged. "I'll have to get my watch adjusted to local time." He searched for the computer readout on the screen beside the door. It showed five zero three. Pressing his watch against the screen, he said, "Synchronize time."

It took only a moment. "Time synchronized." The computer advised him with a pleasant female voice.

He glanced at the watch, satisfied when he saw the numbers matched the ones on the screen. Then he looked at Peters. "What time does the kitchen open?"

"It is open now. Meals are usually served between five and seven."

"Well, let's go then. I'm starving."

They walked back into the first bubble and headed for a building Stonewall hadn't seen before. It turned out to be the kitchen and mess hall. Some of the tables were already occupied. Peters waved to a group of men sitting at the second table.

Stonewall studied the two women behind the serving counter and had to agree with Peters. They would never win any beauty contests, but they seemed capable of doing their job as they efficiently and with a smile heaped food onto the trays. The counter looked nice and clean and the food steaming hot.

"You're new here," the first woman said to Stonewall.

He nodded and gave her a friendly smile. "How did you know?"

She smiled back. "I know every guy on this base." She bent forward and whispered. "If you ever feel lonely, come to the women's quarters and ask for Orina. That's me. I'll keep you company for a while. And believe me, it does get lonely here." She looked at Peters. "You too. My door is always open."

Peters grinned. "So I've heard."

She made a face. "Don't believe everything you've heard, smart guy." Then she chuckled. "But on the other hand, maybe you should."

"Thanks for the invitation," Stonewall said. "I'll think about it."

The second woman winked at him. "Hi. I'm Melina. What do they call you?"

"Stonewall." He studied her casually. She wasn't bad-looking, he decided.

Nice figure. I guess in a pinch I could overlook her thick, wide lips and overbite.

"Stonewall?" she repeated. "I like it. Nice, strong name." Her teeth flashed white in her freckled face. "Don't be a stranger. I'd like to welcome you properly. Make your stay on this hellhole a bit more pleasant."

"Thank you," he said. Shaking his head and chuckling quietly, he followed Peters. *Things have changed more than I thought since my last tour of duty.*

The four men at the table Peters headed for looked up and gave Stonewall a nod.

"Watch out for that one. Her pussy has more teeth than a carnosaur," one of them said, laughing. Then he noticed the bar on Stonewall's sleeve. He stiffened in his seat. "Sorry, sir, I didn't mean to sound…chummy, Master Scout." He threw a glance at Peters. "You could have warned me," he said with an accusing tone.

Stonewall smiled. "Forget about my rank. I've never been one for rules and regulations. Think of me as one of the guys."

"Thank you, Master Scout."

"And don't call me Master Scout, please. I'm Stonewall." He took his seat and looked at his plate. "I hope it tastes as good as it smells and looks. I've been eating too much gruel for these last few months."

"They may not be the best-looking women, but they know how to cook. Among other things." The man chuckled. "By the way, I'm Barry Sanchez." Then he pointed at the other three men. "The guy with the mousy mustache is Felix Morano. The short one is Paul Tsang, and last but not least I'd like to present Greg Erickson. We've nicknamed him 'The Giant' because of his size."

Erickson laughed good-humoredly. His blue eyes twinkled. "I'm barely seven feet tall. There are bigger men out there," he said with a rumbling voice.

Stonewall, who stood six-one, grinned. "There are but I haven't met many with shoulders as wide as yours. I feel like a dwarf against you."

"We all do," Tsang said. "Don't feel bad." He chuckled. "Of course, I always feel like a dwarf."

The other men laughed.

Stonewall felt an instant liking to these men. Maybe his stay would turn out pleasant after all. He dug into his food and found it delivered what it promised. "This is good," he commented. "Too bad we have to drink water instead of beer."

"Beer?" Peters asked. "I was under the impression you didn't drink alcohol. Well, well…it seems there is hope for you yet." He looked around the table. "We're about to get company. Stonewall tells me the Union is sending two hundred soldiers to Epsilon."

"Really?" Morano raised his eyebrows. "Can't say I'm surprised. On my last visit to Star City, I spoke to a couple of miners. They told me that the *Uur* have been attacking spore-miners. Maybe they're getting frustrated and asked for protection." His dark eyes rested on Stonewall. "Am I getting warm?"

"Not really." Stonewall looked at the men. "I shouldn't be

discussing this with you, but I see no harm in it. You'll find out sooner or later. A Spider battleship is sitting at the edge of this system. The Spiders are disputing our claim on Epsilon. They want us gone."

"Are they mad?" Sanchez asked. "We've been here for over twenty years. We've barely begun colonizing the planet. They can't demand and expect everyone leave. We won't take that lying down!"

"We won't," Stonewall said. "That's why the Union sends its own warship. The *Jupiter*, a Class seven Dreadnought, is already on its way."

"That should put some fear into those *Webspinners*," Sanchez said.

"Let's hope. We know very little about them and what they're capable of," Stonewall warned. "The reptilian races keep their distance from the Spiders. So do the Crows. Maybe they have reason to fear them. We are relative newcomers to the Space Community, the new kids on the block. We don't want our noses bloodied by messing with the wrong people."

"By people you mean the Spiders?" Peters chuckled. "I wouldn't exactly call them *people*."

"What would you call them?"

"Pumpkins with hairy legs. How dangerous can they be?"

Everyone laughed again.

"I ran into them on *Fortune*, an unexplored planet in the *Silica System*. One of their exploration shuttles went down in the desert. The Union sent me to lead a rescue team and check for survivors. We did find the stranded shuttle, but the Spiders didn't even let us come close. Two of them met us with weapons in their hands and told us to leave the area immediately. They had not requested our help and wouldn't need it. If you ask me, they looked pretty intimidating. I wouldn't call them pumpkins on legs." Stonewall sipped from his glass. Putting it down, he smiled thinly. "I think we need to tread carefully around them and not rattle our sabers too much. Nobody wants a war with the Spiders."

ABOUT THE AUTHOR

Herbert lives near Winnipeg, Canada. He spends his free time spinning tales about imaginary worlds and the strange creatures inhabiting them. His first published story `The Anniversary Gift' appeared in `Sweet Revenge' published by Midnight Showcase. Even though he writes in other genres, his love is Science Fiction. He enjoys building alien worlds and societies. Most of his stories contain an element of Erotica. All of his books are available from Melange Books.

Website: www.fictitioustales.weebly.com
Blog: hegro.blogspot.com
Blog: hergros.blogspot.com
Email: hegro@shaw.ca

ALSO BY HERBERT GROSSHANS

NOVELS
Bullet of Revenge
A Matter of Justice
Mark of the Cobra
Orola
Orion

RHODAR SERIES
Clouds Over Maridaan

OPERATION STARGATE SERIES
Codename Salamander

SEEDS OF CHAOS DUOLOGY
Eden's Gate
Hell's Gate

STARDOGS DUOLOGY
Return to Redsky
Redemption

Stars in Chains Duology

Slave

Liberator

Web of Conspiracy Trilogy

Death of a Hero

Traitors and Patriots

Tarnished Valor

The Xandra Series

Daughter of the Dark

Mother of Light

Goddess of Life

Lure of Seduction

Escape from Paradise

Iceworld

Alien World

Dark World

Short Story Collections

Dual Visions

Tapestry of Dreams

Time Flares